Seasonal Tales

A Collection of Short Stories

Christie Walker Bos

ISBN: 979-8-9997952-1-2 (e-book)
ISBN: 979-8-9997952-0-5 (paperback)

ACKNOWLEDGEMENTS

Every book is a team effort. Special thanks to Tami Walker for her meticulous proofreading. To Robbie Bos for his creative cover design, and for coming up with the title for this collection of short stories. This is the second time my husband has named one of my books. Good job, babe.

TABLE OF CONTENTS

INTRODUCTION

Authors are often asked, "Where do your stories come from?" My stories seem to pop up like worms after a hard rain or mushrooms pushing up from the underground darkness of my soul. They come late at night, early in the morning, while I'm waiting for a light to change, while I'm sitting at the doctor's office. Anything can spark a story, especially a short story. For example, I was staying at my mother's house when I heard this odd noise at 7 in the morning. Mom was still in bed, and there shouldn't have been anyone else in the house. It turned out to be the robotic vacuum making its rounds. This became the inspiration for the short story, The Machines Awaken.

The micro fiction stories that kick off each season, are a fun challenge … telling a story in exactly 151 words.

I thoroughly enjoyed writing the four short stories for the collection called *Big Bear Tales*, and found I had more stories to tell. I hope you enjoy this collection of *Seasonal Tales*.

WINTER

Julia had sipped sparkling juice while everyone around her rang in the New Year with champagne. Last night was full of laughter, music and the boom of fireworks over the city, the next morning, quiet and still.

Sitting on the edge of the bed, wrapped in a thick bathrobe, Julia watches the first storm of the New Year blanket the front lawn in white. Her hand rests on her swollen belly, caressing the curve as she speaks to the child inside.

"It's your time, your year. Come out, come out, wherever you are."

A small sound, like the popping of a cork from a miniature champagne bottle, precedes the release of a gush of warm fluid.

Julia's eyes go wide in surprise.

Ten hours later, a first daughter is born to a first daughter, on the first day of the year. They name her, Primrose, the first flower to bloom.

Ω

THE SANTA CODE

Exhaling as he folds himself in half, Nick spreads his legs until his round belly drops between his knees, allowing him to pull on the stiff black boots.

"I need to eat better. Maybe that Mediterranean diet …"

Then with a soft chuckle, he discards the idea like a used toothpick. Dieting during the holidays … what a foolish endeavor. Best save the diets for New Year's resolutions.

Boots on, Nick straightens, arching his back to relieve the ball of tension at the base of his spine. One day he'd be too old for this gig, but not today. Pushing himself off the bench, he walks to the rack of cheap red coats. He longs for his rich burgundy robe trimmed in brilliant white fur still in mint condition after hundreds of years of use. The store, however, insists all their

Santas dress alike to perpetuate the myth that there is only one Santa. What a silly notion, he thinks.

Scratchy coat on, Nick sucks in his belly. He forces the metal prong into the last hole of the wide black belt before letting out a relieved sigh. Standing in front of the full-length mirror, Nick scrutinizes his outfit for flaws. Finding none, he reaches for the final pieces of the charade … the itchy white wig and the curly white beard. Silently, he says goodbye to his actual beard, a thick wavy mass that falls off his chin and lands on his chest like freshly falling snow. It doesn't seem right to cover his natural beard in favor of the shoddy synthetic imitation, but he does.

Securing the beard with hooks over his ears, then hiding everything with the equally annoying mane of curly white hair and the traditional Santa hat, Nick reviews the finished "product." Pulling on one white glove and then the other, Nick runs through his mental checklist. Twinkly eyes, check. Merry dimples, check. He pinches his cheeks. Cheeks like roses, check. Cherry nose … close enough. Broad face and round belly, check and check. Seeing himself dressed this way always makes him laugh, causing his belly to shake like a bowl full of jelly, leaving a satisfied grin that curls his droll little mouth up like a bow.

Ho, ho, ho is for amateurs, he thinks.

Before exiting, he reads the list taped to the back of the door. The Santa Code … the Ten Commandments of department store Santas. Nick finds it quite telling that the first item needs to be: *Santa never uses drugs, alcohol, or smokes.* No drinking after Thanksgiving is Nick's motto. But after the 25th, all bets are off. Sitting in front of a crackling fire, feet up, a snifter of brandy to warm his belly as a circle of pipe smoke floats above his head is Nick's reward after one endless night.

Santa always has good hygiene. Someone should point this out to Charlie who smells like day-old fish, Nick thinks, a soft, not unkind chuckle escaping his lips. Not everyone has a kind-hearted woman who does his laundry and points him to the shower when he gets too ripe.

Santa is jolly and happy. Each day, as he walks to the store through the city streets, Nick watches the homeless wander like ghosts, unseen and forgotten. It makes being "jolly" a chore, leaving him longing for the cold north, where no one is left outside alone.

Santa is punctual. They can have perfection or punctuality, but not both, Nick chuckles, knowing there is only one day a year that he's on time.

The next two items: *Santa never displays inappropriate behavior or language*, and *Santa should maintain liability insurance*, have Nick shaking his head.

"Seriously? What is the world coming to?"

Nick closes his eyes and presses his gloved hand to the Code, before opening the door. The glow from the fake snow beckons him to Santa's Village, complete with animatronic reindeer, and bored young women dressed as elves who usher the children up the stairs to meet their idol.

Squeals of delight greet him as he approaches the crowd of children and adults—his second-most favorite moment of the day. He lets out a hearty chuckle, gives a wink and a nod to one of the elves, then climbs the stairs to his golden throne.

***

Nick's eager stride belies the fact that his lower back pulses with pain after sitting on that uncomfortable chair for hours. The orange glow of a campfire flickering from the top of a steel barrel draws Nick like a moth to a flame while the rhythmic squeak of the shopping cart's wonky right wheel alerts the dark shadows of his approach. As he moves closer, the shadows coalesce into men and women warming their hands over the fire, who step aside to make space for Nick and his "sleigh."

"He's here," someone announces from the shadows.

Above the crackling and popping of burning wood, the sound of tent flaps and plastic sheets being pulled aside creates a stir like the rustle of dry leaves.

Within minutes, Nick is surrounded by faces illuminated by the warm glow of the fire and something else … hope.

No one steps closer. No hands grab for the items in the cart. A young girl in a blue hoodie, at least three sizes too large, looks up at Nick with eyes as wide and bright as the full moon. Nick digs into the cart, finally pulling out a pink puffy jacket and a golden hair doll. Bending down, he helps the child into the jacket and hands her the doll.

"Thank you, Santa," the girl says, barely above a whisper, clutching the doll to her chest.

He doesn't need to wear a red suit or a fake beard for the girl to recognize who he is, which makes *this* his favorite moment of the day. Nick passes out blankets and warm clothing, a few more toys, and finally, canned food, until the silver cart stands empty, glistening like tinsel on a tree. Someone wants to keep the shopping cart. He shrugs. He can find another.

Then, with a wink of his eye and a nod of his head, Nick leaves the warmth of the fire and disappears back into the darkness. An hour later, he arrives at a different encampment with another shopping cart filled with hope. Nicolaus Klaas lives by his own Santa Code; no liability insurance needed.

Ω

RESOLUTIONS

The countdown had begun. Ten, nine, eight, seven … Ashly, Emily, and Sara hold their champagne glasses up high. Three, two, one.

"Happy New Year," the three women shout, before downing the bubbly then embracing in a three-way hug.

"I can't believe another year has gone by," Ashly says to her friends, as Auld Lang Syne plays in the background. "This year went by so quickly. It seems like it was only yesterday we were celebrating the New Year."

"Right?" Emily agreed.

"As a kid, I thought time moved so slowly. It took forever for it to be Christmas morning, or my birthday," Emily groans. "Now that I'm old, time flies."

"Old? Forty-two is not old," Sara slurs.

Ashly grabs her friends by the arms. "Let's move somewhere quieter. I can hardly hear you."

Leaving the living room filled with partiers, balloons, and fireworks booming on the giant

11

television, the three friends find a quiet bedroom where a pile of coats covers a queen-sized bed.

Sara opens her arms and lets herself fall backwards on the bed. "I could fall asleep right here, right now."

Emily and Ashly move the coats aside before sitting on the bed on either side of Sara. Emily looks at Ashly over the top of Sara's prone body. "It's a good thing you're driving. Sara is in no condition … yet again. I'm worried about her."

Ashly glances at Sara, who seems to be asleep. "Me, too."

"I'm right here. I can hear you," Sara says without opening her eyes. "Why are you worried?"

"The drinking? Hello?" Emily says, pulling Sara upright so that the three women are sitting side by side on the edge of the bed.

"Oh, that. It's been a tough few days. And it's New Year's Eve, or at least it was a few minutes ago. I'm fine," Sara insists before letting herself fall backwards again, with an "Ahhh" escaping her lips.

Ashly shakes her head. "Same old Sara."

"I'm not old," Sara protests with a hiccup.

"Oh, brother," Emily laughs. "Yes, we are old. My twelve-year-old self would have looked at us like we had one foot in the grave."

"Your twelve-year-old self is a bitch," Sara howls with another hiccup.

"We need to sober her up if we are going to make our resolutions." Ashley stands and disappears into the attached bathroom, coming back with a tall glass of water. "Drink this."

Sara opens an eye. Emily pulls her upright by one arm. She looks at the glass suspiciously. "Where did that glass come from?"

"The bathroom." Ashley holds out the glass.

Sara shakes her head. "I'm not drinking from a glass left in a bathroom. Gross. Do you know that poop particles float in the air after you flush, and they are probably stuck to that glass? I'm not *that* drunk."

"Fine." Ashley leaves the room and returns a few minutes later with a fresh glass filled with water. "This came from a cabinet in the kitchen. Clean enough for you?"

Sara nods and takes the glass, downing the water in long gulps. "Happy?"

"Happier. Want another?" Ashley takes the glass from her hand.

"Sure."

After another glass of water and two aspirins, Sara is ready to talk resolutions. Every year, since they were twelve, Sara, Ashley, and Emily had rung in the New Year together. When they were kids, they drank sparkling apple juice and banged pots and pans together in the street as their parents looked on. One year, Emily's father let them shoot off bottle rockets and dance with sparklers. In high school, they switched the apple juice for beer, and later, when they could afford it, champagne.

After high school, the three girls headed off to different colleges, but they always came home for the holiday break and found a way to celebrate the New Year together. And every year, they made a New Year's Resolution. That was part of the tradition. They decided to write down the resolutions and save them, reviewing them a year later. Ashley had become the Keeper of the Resolutions and never failed to bring them the following year, something both Emily and Sara said they could never do.

"Are we ready?" Ashley asks, her question directed at Sara.

"I'm ready," Sara says, without a hiccup.

Emily nods.

Ashley unzips her mini cross-body evening purse and pulls out three pieces of paper. "Let's review." She unfolds the first scrap. "Let's see. This one is mine. Last year, I resolved to lose 15 pounds and keep it off until tonight." She sighs, then crumples up the paper. "Well, that didn't happen. I think I lost 5 pounds, then gave up."

"As usual," snarks Sara.

"Okay, smarty pants. Let me guess what your resolution was…" Ashley opens the next paper, sets it down, and opens the last one and reads, "I'm going to stop drinking and be totally and completely sober come New Year's Eve, when I will celebrate with one glass of champagne." Ashly looks pointedly at Sara. "How'd that work out for you?"

Sara shrugs. "I think I made it until February, and then it was my birthday, so that was the end of that."

Before Ashley can read the final resolution, Emily snatches it up. "I remember mine. I was going to fix my marriage. As we know, that didn't happen either. So, I guess we all failed … again."

The three women sit in silence, as the muffled sound of the partygoers filters through the door.

Emily crumples her paper and throws it at the wall. "This is ridiculous. I don't think there has been one time, we've all made it a year without breaking our resolution. Why do we bother?"

"Because it's tradition. It's what we do," Sara offers.

"Emily is right. Why make a resolution we know we aren't going to keep," Ashley agrees.

"Maybe if we put some money on it," Sara suggests. "Maybe that would be an incentive to try a bit harder."

"How much money?" Emily wants to know.

"A lot. It would have to be a lot," Ashley adds.

"Yes. A lot," Sara agrees.

"What's a lot to you guys?" Emily asks. "Because after my divorce, I'm on a tight budget."

"What if we each put two hundred—" Ashly starts.

"No! Make it five hundred," Sara cries.

"Too much. How about three hundred," Emily suggests.

"Okay. Three hundred each. If you keep your resolution for the entire year, you get your three hundred back. If you don't, your three hundred goes to those who did. Agreed?" Ashley looks at her two friends, who are nodding.

"Do we have to pay now?" Emily wants to know.

Sara shakes her head. "No. We'll pay up this time next year, but we have to write our resolutions now, just like before. And Ashley will keep them safe like always. Right?"

Ashley nods before pulling out three small sheets of paper. One pink, one orange, and one turquoise.

"Ooooh. Pretty. I want the orange one," Sara says, snatching the piece of paper from Ashley's hand.

Ashley holds out the other two sheets. "Pick."

"Do you care what color?" Emily asks. Ashley shakes her head. Emily picks the turquoise sheet.

Ashley pulls three colored pens that match the paper from her purse.

Emily takes the turquoise pen. "You went all out this year. Colored paper, colored pens. You must have known this year would be different."

"Not really. The company had a special event, and paper and pens were left over."

Sara laughs. "Stolen office supplies. I like it. Can I keep the pen?"

"Whatever," Ashley sighs, wanting to get this over with.

Minutes later, Emily and Sara hand Ashley their folded papers. Ashley adds their resolutions to hers and slips them into her purse.

"How do you not lose them each year or remember where you've put them?" Sara wants to know.

"I keep them in this purse for the entire year. It's my New Year's Eve bag. I only use it for New Year's."

"And here I thought you were too cheap to buy a new purse," Sara laughs.

"Let's see who is laughing next year when I take your three hundred dollars. Maybe I'll even buy a new party purse with the money," Ashley says with a smile, giving Sara a gentle shove that sends her falling onto the bed.

***

Three quick knocks precede the opening of Ashley's front door. Emily sticks her head inside. "Ready or not, here we come."

Ashley's voice comes from somewhere in the house. "Come in. I'm in the kitchen."

Sara and Emily walk in, each carrying a bag, and head to the kitchen. Emily sets her bag on the counter. "Orange chicken, egg rolls, white AND brown rice, chow mein with pork, and of course, fortune cookies."

Ashley pulls her head out of the refrigerator, turning to greet her friends. "Perfect. I'm starving."

Sara sets her bag on the counter and pulls out two bottles of sparkling apple juice. "Just like when we were kids," she says, handing the bottles to Ashley, who places them in the refrigerator before closing the door.

"I'm so glad you guys are here. For some reason, I didn't want to go to a big party this year. I thought it would be better if it were just us."

"Agreed." Sara steps forward and hugs Ashley. "Just like back in the day, right?"

"Right," Emily agrees.

"Coats and purses can go in the guest room down the hall, then join me in the living room. I have appetizers set out."

The three friends spend the evening catching up, eating, laughing, and about once an hour, someone asks, "Can we look at our resolutions?" to which Ashley says, "No. We have to wait until midnight."

With the television tuned to the ball drop in Times Square, the countdown finally begins. Champagne and the sparkling apple juice fill three crystal flutes. When Sara isn't looking, Emily tilts her head toward Sara and raises her eyebrows. Ashley mouths the words, I know, and smiles.

"Five, four, three, two, one. Happy New Year!" the three friends cheer, clinking their glasses together as horns honk and fireworks explode on the television.

After they hug, Sara can't hold it in anymore. "Get your purse, Ashley. I can't wait a second longer."

"Okay. Everyone, place your cash on the table. I'll get the papers."

Sara turns to Emily. "This is so exciting. What was your resolution?"

"You'll know soon enough," Emily says with a twinkle in her eye.

Ashley returns with her party purse and pulls out the three pieces of colored paper. "Who's first?"

Sara's hand flies up. "Me. Me."

"Boy, someone's excited. I'm guessing you kept your resolution, or you wouldn't be so excited," Emily says, bumping shoulders with Sara.

Ashley unfolds the orange piece of paper and reads it to Emily and Sara. "I know I'm a bit tipsy right now, and I know I have a problem, so this year is going to be different. Instead of saying I'm going to quit drinking, my resolution is going to be to join AA, attend meetings. I'm not going to promise success, but I resolve to start the process."

Ashley looks up at her friend, who is beaming. "Wow. That is a great resolution, and to think you wrote that while you were drunk. Amazing."

"And … how did it go?" Emily wants to know.

Sara digs in her pocket and pulls out a dark blue metal chip, holding it out for her friends to see. "This is my 6-month sober chip."

"Oh, Sara. That is wonderful," says Emily.

Ashley jumps up and hugs Sara. "I'm so proud of you. You did it."

"It's a process. I'll never be 'done', but at least I'm on my way and have a support system. I had a one-month chip, then relapsed, had a three-month chip, relapsed again, but this one," she said, holding the chip up high so it caught the light. "This one is the best so far."

"And … as a bonus … you get to keep your three hundred dollars," Ashley says. "Okay, do you want to go next, Emily?"

Emily shakes her head. "I want to go last."

Ashley picks up her wad of cash and counts out one hundred and fifty for Emily and one hundred and fifty for Sara. "I failed … again."

"Wait. You have to read your resolution," Sara says, trying to hand the money back.

"Fine." Ashley doesn't even bother opening her paper. "I wanted to lose 15 pounds and keep it off. I had lost ten by August, but then … some old story … takes eight months to lose 10 and only two weeks to gain it back. It's hopeless." Ashley's head drops to her chest.

"You can't do it on your own," Sara tries. "You need something like AA but for food. You know how many times I've tried to stop drinking. Their 12-step program works."

Emily puts her arm around Ashley's shoulder. "It's not a big deal. Really. Here," she says, and tries to hand back the money. "I don't need your money."

Ashly refuses. "Nope. A deal is a deal. I'll try again this year. Maybe talk to a doctor or something. I don't know, but you are right about one thing: I can't do it alone."

To divert the attention, Ashly pulls out the turquoise paper. Emily puts up her hand like a stop sign.

"Before you read it, I want to explain. Remember how you guys told me my 'picker' was broken?"

"Not really," Ashley admits.

"Oh, I remember. It was after your second divorce, Kevin. What a loser. Then you went on to Charlie, a step up, but not much better. You definitely have a broken picker," Sara says, taking a sip of her sparkling apple juice. "So, what was your resolution?"

Emily signals to Ashley to read her resolution.

Ashley unfolds the turquoise square and reads. "I, Emily, resolve to …" She turns to Emily and comments, "So very formal," then continues reading, "stop dating for an entire year until I figure out what I want in the perfect partner, and only then, will I date again."

"Wow. That's huge," Sara says. "Did you do it, or will I be receiving another 150 dollars?"

Emily grabs her money and stuffs it in her back pocket. "No money for you. I did it."

"Seriously. This entire year? Not one date? Not one … 'let's get coffee' with the cute guy in the cubicle across from yours?" Ashey probes.

"Nope. Not one. And … I figured out what I want. So," she says to Sara, "No money for you."

"And what did you figure out?" Sara asks, scooting forward on her seat. "You've been batting for the wrong team?" she says, sarcasm dripping from her lips.

"Sort of," Emily admits with a wicked smile.

"No way," Ashley protests. "You're a lesbian!"

"Not that there is anything wrong with that," Sara adds, punching Ashley in the arm.

"No, of course not. It's fine. But how did we, your best friends, not know this? How did YOU not know this?"

"Whoa. You're getting ahead of yourselves here," Emily says. "I've switched species."

Sara looks at her glass of bubbly. "Did someone replace my juice with champagne, because I just heard you say you switched species. What does that even mean?"

"I'm in love …"

Sara and Ashley hold their breath and lean in, waiting.

"With my new … puppy!"

"A dog?" Ashley squeals, then turns to Sara. "It's a dog. She's in love with her dog."

"Oh, thank god," Sara says, "I thought we were going to need to find a support group for people with weird fetishes."

"Want to see a picture? Her name is Lady, and she's the cutest. She's staying with my mom tonight. I thought of bringing her, but then it would have ruined the surprise." Emily found her phone and shared a dozen images of Lady, a Cocker Spaniel. "She is the love of my life. With her, I don't think about being alone, I'm not alone. And she loves me unconditionally. She cuddles with me at night and gives me kisses in the morning. She's absolutely perfect in every way," Emily gushes.

"Isn't Lady the name of the dog in the Disney movie, *The Lady and the Tramp*?" Ashley asks.

"Yes. And it's the same breed, too. I just had to name her Lady."

"I guess that makes you, the Tramp," Sara teases.

"I guess it does," Emily laughs.

Ω

THE PAINTING

The painting spoke to me the first time we walked into the counselor's office. Not like a creepy ghostly voice or anything. It called out to me, beckoned me in, touched a hidden memory. Too much? Maybe. Okay, so it spoke to me.

On our first visit, Dr. Marion Davis welcomes us with handshakes and directs us with an outstretched arm to have a seat on the long blue sofa. I wedge myself into the left corner. Timothy pauses, calculating the optics … sit next to me pretending we still liked each other, take the opposite corner to indicate we hated each other's guts, or plop down in the middle and let the doctor sort it all out. He chooses the middle, stretching his arms across the top of the couch like a condor drying its feathers in the noonday sun. The tips of his fingers are close enough to touch my shoulder if he wants to. He doesn't want to.

While Dr. Davis collects a pad off her desk and settles herself into what looks like a very comfortable, overstuffed chair, I look around. Finding a decorative pillow on a chair next to the end table, I snatch it up and place it on my lap, resting my crossed arms on the pillow. In front of us, on a low, modern coffee table sits a porcelain bowl filled with wrapped caramels and two boxes of tissues—one directly in front of me and the other at the opposite end. Timothy spots the candy, tucks his wings and disengages from the couch to grab a massive handful, dumping the candy into his lap. I guess he wants to make sure he doesn't go hungry in the next hour or more likely, he's making sure to lay claim to the loot before Dr. Davis or I can eat them all, leaving him nothing. Growing up, he was the youngest of six kids and apparently had to fight for his dinner like a wolf puppy.

I cut my eyes at him. He responds by throwing his hands in the air and with a whine I've grown to hate asks, "What?" I shake my head and roll my eyes to the ceiling, where I find a smiley face sticker.

Must be for patients who choose to lie on this couch. My gynecologist tried a similar trick, taping pictures of kittens over the exam table. Who doesn't like looking at adorable kittens while a doctor pokes around in your hoo-ha?

When I look to Dr. Smith for support, she takes his side. "It's okay. That's what they're there for. I have a whole bag."

"Ha! See," gloats Timothy.

The doctor turns to Timothy. "Most people only take one, two at the most, but it's fine," Dr. Smith says with what I imagine is a forced smile.

Timothy is at least aware enough to look embarrassed, although he doesn't return any of the candy. I feel vindicated. One point for me, although I'm not supposed to keep score but in my mind I do. I just don't say it out loud anymore.

"Let's get started."

Here we go.

This isn't our first rodeo. We went to a counselor two years into our marriage, then two years later, and now we're back. We talk and talk, never saying anything different or getting to the heart of the problem. According to him … we don't have enough sex, (I wish someone would give me the official definition of "enough" because to Timothy it means whenever he's in the mood.), I treat him like a child (because he acts like one … Exhibit A, taking all the candy), I look down on him because he doesn't make as much money as I do (which is true, not the looking down on him part, but the making more money part) and I'm a lousy housekeeper (also true, but I don't remember, 'cleaning, cooking, and laundry' being part of our wedding vows.)

My complaints go toe-to-toe with his. All he ever wants to do on the weekend is lay around (He's tired from working all week. I work, too, but it's not physically exhausting like construction work, he reminds me every chance he gets.) He wants to have sex two to three times a week, whether or not I'm in the mood, which I'm not. Foreplay is a foreign word to him. His idea of "getting me in the mood" is to crack open a beer and hand it to me. So romantic. Sometimes, he'll buy a bunch of flowers from a corner vendor on his way home from work, which I used to think was a lovely gesture until I discovered it came with expectations attached.

His boyish good looks have allowed him to get away with acting like a child. It worked on me … at first. But the curtain has been drawn aside to reveal someone who hasn't figured out how to be an adult, and I don't want to be the one to teach him. He assumed, once we were married, that I would take over all the household chores … dusting, vacuuming, laundry, grocery shopping, making dinner. I thought (Silly me) that we would split up the jobs, since we both work, but when I remind him that I have a job, too, he accuses me of throwing my job in his face, making him feel less of a man, blah, blah, blah.

Counseling helps for a while, since we can both vent in a safe environment, promise to do better, try harder. But we seem to be in a two-year cycle … pissed off, counseling, working on it, then back to being pissed off again because nothing has changed.

I zone out as Timothy fills this new doctor in on our history, then launches into his complaints. It probably seems like I'm listening intently, nodding intermittently as I seem to be watching Dr. Smith scribble her useless notes. What I'm actually doing is studying the painting on the wall behind her.

The pastoral scene of a dirt road disappearing around a corner into the distance draws me in. There is something familiar about it, about the style, the place. It's like I've been there before. On either side of the road are blobs of color meant to represent foliage, in various shades of green. Two rows of trees, flank the road. The trees are tall, and thin, pointed at the top like a pencil. I can't remember their name, but I think they are Italian or something. And just as the road begins to bend to the left and disappear, there is a hill, and on the hill, a red farmhouse, or at least it looks like it's supposed to be a building of some sort. I know I've been on this road before, I've seen that farmhouse or barn, but where? I'm flipping through memories in my mind when Dr. Smith breaks into my revelry.

"Kim, do you have something you'd like to add?" she tries.

I'm not taking the bait. "Nope. I think he's covered everything." Turning to Timothy. "Good job, dear."

All he hears are the words, "Good job." The sarcasm is lost on him.

"I see," she says, before jotting something on her pad.

Probably using words like, "shut off," "uncommunicative," maybe even, "hostile."

"Now you know what I have to deal with," Timothy says, before filling in my silence with more of his insights into what's wrong with me, the marriage, my attitude, the state of the world, concluding with a story about work. Always something about work, the most interesting place on earth.

Timothy is like a human juke box of words. Insert a quarter and he'll keep talking and talking. The only way to stop him is to unplug him. The only thing I've found that can "unplug him" is having sex, which has become the only reason we have sex at all … I just want him to shut up.

Of course, I've never admitted this to Timothy or a counselor, or anyone else for that matter. The question I keep asking myself … "How did I end up here?" bounces around in my head. Not as in here, here, the counselor's office, but here, married to this man I don't even like. He's not a terrible person. He doesn't beat me, steal my money, or even leave his underwear on the floor. He's an okay roommate and maybe if we'd stayed roommates, it would have worked out. It's the damn sex. I'm honestly not interested … in the least, and it seems that's all he's interested in. It's like he thinks our vows guaranteed unlimited sex for the rest of his life.

What I am interested in is the painting.

Time's up. Timothy gathers his candy and stuffs the pieces into his jean pockets before standing. The doctor is saying something about seeing us next week at the same time. I interrupt her.

"Tell me about that painting."

She seems confused about my question, so I repeat. "The painting. Behind your desk. Can I take a closer look?"

I see her glancing at the large clock on the wall before answering. "Sure. I have another appointment at three."

It's 2:50. "I'll be quick."

Stepping around her desk, I stand two feet away. Close enough to look for an artist signature. Nothing. I lean in and discover much of the perceived depth of the painting comes from the heavy application of paint. It's thick. What I thought were deliberate shadings are miniature peaks and valleys of paint where shadows hide.

"Whoever painted this used a ton of paint. It's so thick," I exclaim. Something about this particular technique noodles at the edge of my consciousness.

"Come on," Timothy hails from the open door. "I want to stop at the store on the way home. We're out of beer."

Reluctantly, I step back, letting my eyes travel the dirt road one last time, before turning and walking out.

The doctor calls after me. "See you next week."

"Yes," I tell her. She probably thinks I'm coming back to work on my marriage, but what I will be returning for is to look at that painting.

***

At the conclusion of our second visit, I again take a moment to examine the painting. "Do you know who the artist is?" I ask Dr. Smith, as I step around the desk to take another look.

"Sorry, I don't."

"Where did you get it?" I want to know.

The doctor shrugs. "I have no idea. My husband bought it for me when I was decorating the office. Says it's soothing to look at. Do you think it's soothing?"

I nod. It's more than that, though. I want, no need, to know where her husband bought the painting.

"Can you ask your husband where he purchased it. I'm interested in finding the artist. Maybe buy something for my office. I do find it soothing," I lied.

"Sure," she says, taking a quick look at the clock on the wall. "I'll let you know next week."

"Thanks."

Joining Timothy in the waiting room he asks, "What's up with your fascination with that stupid painting?"

I bristle at the word "stupid". Of course, because I'm interested in something it's stupid. I don't even bother answering as I walk past him and head to the door.

***

After our third and hopefully last visit, I know where Dr. Smith's husband purchased the painting. On a business trip about an hour away, he'd taken a stroll through a farmers' market and art fair, which by googling, I discovered happens every Friday from 6:00 am to 1:00 pm.

Using a personal day to get the day off, I find myself behind the wheel at nine in the morning, excitement humming through my veins. One morning last week, I woke with a jolt and knew the location portrayed in the painting. I remember walking up the dirt road, holding a warm hand. At the red barn, we stopped and kissed. My first. Tentative at first, both of us unsure what we were doing, our lips lingered, pressed against each other.

My pulse quickens at the memory. I pass through rolling hills of sundried grasses dotted with the occasional deep green of oaks, but no Italian Cypress. (I looked it up.) The location of the barn and dirt road is from my hometown on the other side of the country, making the fact that the painting was purchased here, interesting. Pulling into town, I follow the commands of my GPS. As I draw closer to the park hosting the farmers' market, the traffic picks up. I park three blocks away and walk at a clipped pace, anxious to solve the mystery of how the painting turned up 3,000 miles from where it was painted.

Making my way through the fruits and vegetables stands, ignoring the proffered samples of cut peaches and wedges of blood oranges, I finally arrive at the artisans' booths. My head on a swivel, I walk down the middle of the aisle searching for a booth selling paintings. After walking the length of the first row and finding nothing, I find I'm second guessing myself.

I should have done more research instead of heading off on a wild goose chase. The artist probably isn't here. Maybe someone bought this and now is selling it along with other stuff they've pulled from their garage.

Turning a corner, I head down another row featuring photography, jewelry, and ceramics, but no paintings. One row left.

Halfway down the third row, I see a booth with paintings of a similar style. My footsteps quicken, and I bump into someone.

"Sorry," I say, as I rush to stand in front of a large vertical painting of a single Italian Cypress.

Thick paint in shades of light browns and grays create the straight trunk of the cypress. A patch of paint in the shape of a heart is smooth. Inside the heart, carved into the tree two letters, "K" + "T". This was our tree, our declaration of love. The memories of that summer long ago wash over me like the tide rushing to the shore. Walks up the road holding hands making plans, stolen kisses near the abandoned red barn, carving our initials in the tree and then lying in its shade on a blanket experimenting with touches and feelings, then the crushing moment when my parents announced we were moving across the country. Tearful promises to keep in touch, write letters, make phone calls, all of which dissolved after only six months, much like my memory of that first love, until I saw the painting.

A single finger reaches out to touch the letters, when a voice asks, "Kim?"

Turning, I come face to face with my first love. "Theresa Bennet, as I live and breathe. You're here."

"And so are you," she says, awe causing her voice to float away on the breeze that sends wisps of blonde hair dancing around her face. "How? How did you find me?"

"A painting. Your painting … in an office. I followed the painting, here … didn't expect to find you as well." I look back at our initials carved in the tree. "You've never forgotten."

She shakes her head. "And you, did you forget?"

I look down at my shoes, knowing the answer might hurt, but honesty between us was something we both cherished. "Sorry. I did. I buried everything from that summer deep, covering it with dating boys and eventually a marriage."

"How's that working out for you?" she asks with her trademark smirk, and a single raised eyebrow.

"The business with the painting is a marriage counselor's office," I say with a shrug. "How about you … did you marry, have a partner?"

Her dark chocolate eyes never leave my face as she says, "No. I've been waiting for you."

Ω

I.C.E. I.C.E. BABY

The first "incident," as the press called it, took place on February 12th in New York City's Financial District at 11 Wall Street and 18th Broad Street as the day traders streamed out of the NY Stock Exchange shortly after 4:00 pm Eastern Time.

The mostly white men in suits, were surprised to see two dozen men, wearing what the public now considered standard I.C.E. gear—black balaclavas covering the lower half of their faces, wraparound sunglasses shielding their eyes, a ball cap, camouflage pants, thin, long-sleeved black shirts covered by a tactical vest with a black patch sewn on the back with white letters declaring, "Police I.C.E." They stood in a line along the sidewalk, their backs to a row of black SUVs.

A young man carrying a leather briefcase walked up to one of the agents. "Rounding up the janitorial service?" To his friend standing behind him. "Looks like we'll be emptying our own trash," he said with a smirk.

The agent hissed, "Pendejo," under his balaclava. Two agents stepped forward and grabbed the young man and pushed him to the ground, pulled his arms behind his back, and handcuffed him.

"Hey, what are you doing? I'm a U.S. Citizen. Check my ID. You can't do this. I have rights," he wailed, as his friend looked on in horror.

With the precision of a well-trained military maneuver, agents broke ranks, walked calmly into the crowd of day traders, and picked out their prey, two agents per trader. Some struggled, kicked, swore, and lashed out. Others wore masks of confusion and disbelief as they were cuffed and loaded into the waiting cars. Within fifteen minutes, twelve men were taken, the rest scattering in panic.

Across the country, the same scenario played out in front of Federal buildings, as groups of white males, mostly upper-middle class, found themselves swept up and taken away. When word of the detentions reached the White House, the administration claimed it to be "Fake News." A hoax meant to rile up the people. These are U.S. Citizens; it must be a mistake."

And yet, they all disappeared without a trace. It was no mistake.

***

As Maria Sanchez watches the various news channels on seven different televisions covering the event, a wry smile graces her face as she cracks open a bottle of Pacifico, her legs stretched out, her combat boots on a coffee table. Maria is what they used to call a Dreamer, an undocumented immigrant who was brought to the U.S. as a child. She's still a dreamer, but now she has a different dream in mind … revenge.

Two years ago, Maria's parents were swept up in an I.C.E. raid at a restaurant. Green card holders for the last twenty-five years, currently in the process of becoming U.S. Citizens, their only crime had been being in the wrong place at the wrong time, that and the color of their skin. They died in a detention center known as Alligator Alcatraz. Who knows what happened to their bodies.

In the living room, sitting on sofas, the floor and kitchen chairs, are a collection of "murderers and rapists" if you are to believe the administration. Maria has never felt safer.

Another dreamer, Jose Sanchez, beer in hand, plops on the couch next to Maria. "Mom will come back to haunt you if you don't take your boots off the table."

Maria rolls her eyes but complies.

Suddenly, all the stations switch to an image of the Oval Office. Boos erupt.

"Quiet!" Maria bellows. "Let's hear how he's going to explain this."

Of course he can't explain it. Instead, he blathers on about staying calm and finding the perpetrators. The sound of his voice makes Maria want to vomit. "Turn it off. We have work to do."

***

The first wave of detentions of non-immigrants barely made a blip in the 24-hour news cycle. The second wave was a different matter. Large political donors, the money behind the machine, were targeted. And finally, the sons and daughters of Senators and Congressmen, who supported the administration, were taken from their schools, places of business, and homes. Now, the media, the people, the powers that be, were paying attention.

Conspiracy theories crawled out of the darkness like snails and slugs after a hard rain, with both sides pointing fingers across the aisle. Radical groups were quick to take credit for what they were now calling "kidnappings," which Maria found amusing. Maria's group remained silent. There were no ransom notes, no demands. The message didn't need to be written out … no one is safe.

When immigrants, illegal and legal alike, were "kidnapped," it was called "arrested and detained." When a person was arrested by the police, at least the suspect was assumed innocent until proven guilty. For immigrants, it was the opposite: guilty until proven innocent. Proving your innocence depended on someone hearing your case. Suspected criminals have the right to remain silent, the right to an attorney, and if they couldn't afford an attorney, one would be appointed. Persons arrested and detained by I.C.E. had no such rights and often disappeared into the system, shipped to detention centers, and sometimes out of the country, all sanctioned by the politicians and the courts. Maria's parents never had their day in court.

Modeling her organization after the resistance movement during WWII, information and contacts were compartmentalized. Everyone was on a "need-to-know" basis, even Maria. Detention centers, built thirty miles south of the U.S. border, consisted of the bare basics—temporary shade covers, a bucket of water with a dipper, another bucket for waste, a sleeping pad and blanket, and two meals a day of a thin soup and stale bread. After a week of being detained, the gates swung open, and they were told they were free to go.

The day trader was in the first batch of detainees to be released. Without his cellphone, money, wallet, or ID, he was expected to find his way home. "Go? Go where? I don't even know where I am."

He was handed two jugs of water by a masked guard, who shrugged, pointed, and said one word. "North."

Once everyone left, the camp was dismantled and set up in a new location. Maria knew this strategy wouldn't work for long, once people returned to the U.S. Some of them would try to describe where they had been held, even though they had arrived by bus, hooded and during the night.

Upon reaching the U.S./Mexico border, they were faced with the same obstacles every immigrant meets… a wall, barbed wire, border patrols, and a bureaucracy designed to discourage all.

Back in the U.S., people were panicking. Were the I.C.E. agents on the street here for them? No longer were people safe based on the color of their skin, their political connections, or the size of their bank accounts. And that was the point.

"Now you know how we feel," Maria says to the television, as those returning tell their stories to the media, now suddenly concerned with the fate of people illegally detained. Protests swelled, demanding the end to the entire I.C.E. program. There had been protests before, but this time, the people who were protesting were also threatening to withdraw funding and support, a more powerful tool than millions of people taking to the streets with cardboard signs.

The operation lasted one month. Some of the people released into the unforgiving Sonoran and Chihuahuan Deserts didn't make it, and unsurprisingly, their "captors" were dubbed "murderers," even while their counterparts in the U.S.—with a larger number of deaths on their watch—were not.

The group without an official name, internet presence, or paper trail, vanished like smoke into the wind.

Ten years later, immigration reform looked different. Systems were put in place providing easier pathways to citizenship. Alligator Alcatraz and other inhuman camps were dismantled. Lawyers were provided to those who couldn't afford them to help with the naturalization process, and new laws were enacted to protect the rights of people in the process.

The most famous and oft quoted line from the poem "The New Colossus" by Emma Lazarus, inscribed on a bronze plaque inside the pedestal of the Statue of Liberty … "Give me your tired, your poor, your huddled masses yearning to breathe free," once again rang true.

$$\Omega$$

SPRING

My annual ritual, spring cleaning, has taken over my day with dusting, sweeping, mopping the floors, and now the final chore … vacuuming. Warm afternoon sunlight streams through the windows, casting pools of bright light, creating miniature shadows throughout the shag carpeting.

Before I turn on the vacuum, Buster starts barking. His butt in the air in the downward dog position, he pushes his nose under the coffee table. Down on my knees, I peer under the table for whatever is driving my dog crazy. A squeaky toy, no doubt. Then I see him … Jesus.

Dark hair and beard, an understanding smile. Surely a trick of the light hitting yarn strands of brown and tan? I look away, then back.

"Jesus Christ!"

Should I take a picture? Call a priest? I cross myself, then look again. The light changes. Jesus dissolves. Buster abruptly stops his barking. The miracle departs.

Ω

LIVE LIKE A HUMMINGBIRD ...
BIALTITUDINALLY

Incessant bright sunshine, raging hot wildfires, bursts of cold pouring rain, inundations of thick coffee-colored mud ... locals joke that these are the four seasons found in most of Southern California. To experience real seasonal changes—from spectacular fall foliage to snow-covered pines and air so cold exhalations become visible clouds—Trish decided to take a trip up ... up to the mountains where she discovered a whole new world.

One hundred miles from the beaches of Orange County, Big Bear Valley—with its mountains blanketed in pines, sparkling blue/green lake, and four distinct seasons—became a clarion call, beckoning Trish to move to where the air is clearer, the sky is bluer, and the stars are brighter. And so, she moved, not across the country to another state, but vertically from 89 feet above sea level to 6,752 feet.

After living in Big Bear for a couple of years, Trish became aware of the distinct clues that signal the start of each season. In the mountains, the dull green rabbit brush flowers burst into lemon yellow in September, the first sign that fall is right around the corner. The hummingbirds flit and hover as they siphon nectar from the late blooming fire engine red trumpets of the California fuchsia. Shorter days and less daylight become a red light for the deciduous trees to stop food production causing aspen and cottonwood leaves to change from green to sunshine yellow and maples to show off their fiery red finery before dropping, covering the ground with a multicolored carpet.

As nighttime temperatures plummet and the days grow steadily colder, the hummingbirds disappear, heading down the mountain to warmer climes where flowers still bloom and the sugar water in their feeders doesn't freeze. The mountain population prepares for winter too, by pulling out sweaters, stacking firewood, and firing up snowblowers.

Spring becomes a big deal after being hunkered down for the winter where a thick layer of snow erases the memory of Trish's garden and yard. One of the first signs of spring are the bright yellow daffodils, deep purple hyacinths, and Easter egg-colored tulips that push up through the soil announcing warmer days are on their way. For Trish, the true heralds of spring are the hummingbirds ... like anxious shoppers waiting for the doors to open for a grand opening, they whirl around the spots where Trish hung their feeders in the summer.

For twenty years, Trish watched the seasons change ... the hummingbirds depart, the hummingbirds return. Aching bones, an aging back that protested every time she had to clear her 120-foot driveway of snow, and sore arms from moving firewood from the woodpile to the garage to the living room, had Trish thinking about the hummingbirds and where they went to escape the winter.

"I wish I were a hummingbird," she mused, as she took the feeders down for the winter.

Sitting in front of a blazing fire, Trish began researching. Where did the Big Bear hummingbirds go in the winter. She typed in "vertical migration" to see if there was a word that would describe this movement of animals—including people—who changed elevation with the seasons. She discovered hummingbirds weren't the only ones that migrate up and down. Krill, copepods, and various zooplankton—and the fish that feed on them—move vertically from the ocean depths to the surface waters at night, then move back down during the day. This pattern of movement is called Diel

Vertical Migration or Diurnal Vertical Migration or DVM for short.

"I guess this description would work if I was traveling up and down the mountain daily for a job like Bob next door," she giggled, thinking about the look on Bob's face if she told him he was a Diurnal Vertical Migrant. Bob wouldn't know what "diurnal" meant and would be offended at being called a migrant, making it all the more tempting to tell him the next time she saw him.

Down another rabbit hole she went, looking for the perfect word. She discovered that other large mammals—elk and deer—migrate down the mountain in the winter looking for warmer temperatures and more access to food, returning in the spring and summer. Ah ha. This type of movement was a thing … migrating vertically, but it needed a better name than Diel Vertical Migration. Besides being a mouthful, she couldn't imagine saying, "I'm living a diel vertical migratory lifestyle." Trish decided the world needed a new word, and she would be the one to invent one.

After a bit more research on her phone and another cup of coffee spiked with Baileys Irish Cream, the word came to her … Bialtitudinal! She was so thrilled by the sound of the new word rolling off her tongue that she decided to share it with her friends, especially the ones who left the mountain every fall for the desert.

"I'm thinking of living a bialtitudinal lifestyle," she posted on Facebook and Instagram.

Her mouth turned up at the corners thinking of the raised eyebrows and confused head tilts her post might cause as her friends and family read what she had written.

"From now on, I'll be following the hummingbirds," she added, imagining spreading her wings and flying off the mountain as soon as the temperatures dropped below 50. The very idea warmed her.

Before she clicked on "Post" the all-knowing spellcheck police underlined "bialtitudinal" with an ugly red squiggle declaring it incorrect and then tried to come up with the "correct" word for her obvious misspelling. Trish had to add the word to her personal dictionary to make spellcheck stop harassing her. Honestly, spell check can be so annoying! she thought.

"All words are made up by someone, at some point," she said with an air of superiority to her phone as she clicked Post.

Trish's new word had its roots in words such as bicoastal, bilingual, and biannual. All these words mean "two" of something such as two coasts, two languages, or two times a year. Since Trish made up the word, it was her privilege to make up the definition.

Bialtitudinal (bī·altə·to□odənəl) *adjective*

1. living at, taking place in, or involving two altitudes.

There. It's official, she thought, deciding to post the definition as well, including the following sentence. "Hummingbirds and people who summer in the mountains and winter in the desert, migrating vertically … up the mountain, down the mountain, live a bialtitudinal lifestyle or live bialtitudinally!"

With an air of satisfaction, Trish added another log to the fire, refilled her coffee and added a bit more Baileys in celebration of her inevitable stardom at inventing a new word. She imagined social media blowing up with hundreds, no thousands of likes for her new word. After all, Big Bear alone had a huge population of bialtitudinal migrants, spending November – April off the mountain in the desert or at the beach, returning in May to enjoy the glory of spring and the relatively cooler summer temps that come with living over a mile high. Trish imagined other locales where people migrated up and down, all of them embracing her new word.

The phone rang, startling her out of her revery. Her son had seen her post and called to see if she was feeling well.

"You're bi? You want to be a hummingbird? What's going on?" he asked, concern making his normally deep voice an octave higher.

Was it the Baileys or her son thinking she was coming out of the closet as a bisexual hummingbird that started her laughing so hard, she almost peed her pants. Gasping for breath, Trish managed to say, "I'm fine" before another seizure of giggles erupted.

***

This was Trish's second year living in the desert for the winter. Last winter, her back had rejoiced, her tan never faded, and she had lost a few pounds since she was able to garden, walk, and golf year-round. A hummingbird hovered outside the kitchen window where she had hung the feeder the winter before.

"All right, all right," she said to the impatient jeweled marvel, as she mixed the sugar water.

Trish would have liked to have said that this was a *bialtitudinal* hummingbird, down from the mountains for the season, just like her. But without attaching a teeny tiny tracking device to his needle-thin leg, she really couldn't say for sure.

What she did know was that the hummingbirds had it right all along … head down for the winter, back up for the summer. Guess there is something to be said for being a bird brain after all.

Ω

A NEW LOVE

Death by a thousand cuts ... that's how she thought of her relationship with her husband, Hewey. Tiny, little slices, delivered day after day, year after year, that have left her love for her husband bleeding out, drip by drip.

It hadn't always been this way, or maybe more accurately, she hadn't noticed, what with dual careers and raising children. Now, being retired empty nesters meant there were no distractions, no excuses, nothing left but the two of them and she couldn't help but notice.

A birthday or anniversary missed ... no biggie. She would remind him, make the plans. What hurt was the lack of effort on his part. She knew he was more than capable of planning something as evidenced by his elaborate fishing vacations with their sons or organizing and executing the two major tournaments for his bowling league. When it came to his wife, however, he didn't seem interested in applying these skills for her. In his totem pole of priorities, where he sat perched at the top like a magnificent bald eagle, she squatted at the bottom, with everything from the kids, bowling buddies and perfect strangers balanced above her.

For forty years, she'd asked him to please place his dirty laundry in the hamper, not on the bathroom floor surrounding the hamper. It didn't matter to him that this bothered her. He couldn't do this small thing, even when it was the cause of more arguments than she could count. Cut.

When it came to picking a movie for the evening, she often asked, "What do you want to watch?" He never reciprocated asking her what she wanted to watch. When she managed to pick the movie, he wouldn't join her, like she joined him. Cut.

After years of making his dinner, he never asked, "What would *you* like for dinner?" It wasn't that he didn't know how to cook. He did, but he always made something he wanted to eat, even when he knew she couldn't eat it (lactose intolerant). "Oh yeah, you don't eat cheese," Hewey would say, as if this was new information. When it came to details about her, he couldn't make the effort to remember. Cut.

He could talk on and on about what happened at bowling league or on the fishing trip with the boys but never asked her what she'd been up to for the week he'd been gone. The only conclusion she could come to … he didn't care. Cut.

Once in a while, he would ask, "How was your day?" as he walked through a room on his way to somewhere else, never pausing long enough to hear her answer. Cut.

And then there were the deeper cuts. The pointed pokes, little jabs he saved for when they were at a party with friends or with family around, so she couldn't say anything back or if she did, it made her look like she had thin skin or was starting a fight.

"Relax," Hewey would snap. "I'm joking," he would sneer, adding to her embarrassment. Cut.

He avoided saying these things in the privacy of their home, knowing she would immediately respond, turning the comment into a verbal battle.

She felt unseen, unimportant, and unappreciated. Cut.

Hewey wasn't a bad man in any sense of the word. He wasn't abusive. He did do nice things on occasion, but mostly he ignored her or simply assumed, after all these years, that she was okay with his "quirks" as he called them and continued on with his entrenched patterns of behavior, never making an effort when it came to her, never thinking that someday she would simply bleed out.

None of these "slights" as a counselor once called them (a male counselor) were reasons for a divorce, especially after being married so long. "This waning of affection is to be expected after so long. It's natural," he'd said.

Natural or not, it still hurt, still made her sad. Since her husband had no intention of changing, then it would be up to her to change her situation. But how? She had no clue until she opened the Sunday paper and there it was … big, bold, and beautiful, calling to her like a siren from the sea.

***

Standing in front of the sleek, modern building, Claire climbed the stairs to the grand entrance, anticipation quickening her steps. Through the heavy glass doors and into the foyer she paused to take it all in, the atmosphere … calm, the lightening … subtle, indirect, the surfaces … warm, inviting. Directly in front of her stood a large information desk where several people gathered, all speaking in hushed tones. She approached.

The woman behind the desk asked, "Are you here for the tour?"

Clarie nodded.

The woman handed her a clipboard with a sign-in sheet. "The next tour starts in ten minutes. Feel free to explore on your own until then."

Instead of wandering around, Claire found an empty chair and sank into its cushioned embrace. She watched a group of eight be led away, a slender woman in her forties talking softly as they entered a glass enclosed room off of the foyer. More people entered, approached the information desk, and then joined Claire as they waited for their tour guide. A young man with dark hair pulled back into a low ponytail emerged from a closed door. He conferred with the woman behind the information desk before taking a clipboard and joining the group of waiting people.

"Good morning. My name is Todd and I'll be showing you around starting with the children's library."

The group followed Todd through a set of heavy glass doors to a magical space designed to capture the imaginations of young readers. Opalescent jelly fish with their long wavy tendrils hung from the ceiling over an area with an ocean theme. In another section, plush monkeys hung from vines above soft coconut trees. In all, there were four themed areas, ocean, jungle, space, and famous faces, each with a dozen cozy chairs, beanbag chairs, and couches.

"The children's library is completely separate from the rest of the building, and fairly soundproof. Kids tend to be noisy and while we still encourage quiet, we want the librarians here to help the kids find what interests them, not be disciplinarians, demanding silence. We have a full schedule of events for the kids, including traditional story times, but also small plays and movies that are based on books," Todd explained as he pulled sheets from the clipboard with the schedule for the month of August.

Claire wished her kids were still little. She would have loved bringing them here. Maybe grandkids, if that ever happens, she thought.

Leaving the children's library, they continued their tour, into the stacks, down rows and rows of books, up an elevator to an area that took Claire's breath away. The adult reading room felt like she'd come home. Designed to resemble a living room, complete with a large screen TV that played a continuous loop of a crackling fire, the room had comfortable chairs, sofas, coffee tables, and area rugs, which were all surrounded by books. It even had a coffee and tea station providing everything Claire could want, especially the chance to read, uninterrupted in silence. This would be her escape pod, her home away from home, a place where no one would ask her questions or play music or turn on the television.

Todd stood in front of the television. "This is our adult only reading room. This is your space. For those who have children, you can check them into the children's library and head up here. You may be wondering about the television."

Heads nodded.

"On specific days, this room will be used for special events such as author presentations, multi-media classes, and my favorite, The Movie vs The Book Club. The month prior to the movie being shown, anyone who wants to participate will read the selected book. Our first will be *Gone with the Wind* by Margaret Mitchell. The library will bring in extra copies for the event. Then, we will gather here to watch the movie, followed by a discussion of which was better, the movie or the book."

Sounds wonderful, Claire thought. "How do we sign up?" she asked.

"There's a sign-up sheet at the front desk for this program and several others," Todd answered before passing out another flyer with all the scheduled adult programing.

Looking at the list, Claire's smile widened as she realized she could be gone every day of the week if she wanted.

***

It took almost month for Hewey to notice that Claire wasn't home much, or more specifically, home when he was home. Monday and Thursday evenings, Hewey took off for his bowling leagues and Claire, happy to have the house to herself, stayed home. Tuesdays, Wednesdays and Fridays, Claire left the house after dinner and didn't come home until 9:00 or 9:30. She passed him in the living room watching some Zombie film, saying, "Good night," before she headed upstairs.

Another thing he finally noticed, when he ran out of clean underwear, was his dirty laundry stayed on the bathroom floor. When he mentioned this, Claire informed him that she was only washing clothes that were in the laundry hamper. He hadn't noticed that Claire had moved all of her bathroom products, hairbrush, toothbrush, and makeup to the guest bathroom down the hall. She'd decided that if she didn't use their bathroom, then she wouldn't see the mess and it wouldn't bother her. She'd been right.

One Friday night, after she'd loaded the dishwasher after dinner, grabbed her purse and headed for the front door, Hewey cut her off, standing between her and the door. "Where are you going?" he said with a feigned casual air.

"To the library."

His casual tone slipping. "Really?"

Claire sighed. "Yes, Hewey. Really. I told you before. I belong to a book club that meets on Fridays at the library. Of course, you don't remember that, do you?"

"What about Tuesday and Wednesday nights? You have book club then?"

Claire shook her head. "No. Not on Tuesday and Wednesday." She could see his frustration building but she refused to give him more information. What does he care, she thought.

Taking her sweater off the hook by the door, Claire sidestepped around her husband and left.

The following Saturday, Claire took off before dinner, for the once a month The Movie vs The Book club's screening of *The Shawshank Redemption* based on the Stephen King novella. She'd never seen the movie and had found the book riveting, reading it over the course of two uninterrupted nights at the library.

So engrossed in replaying the book in her mind, she didn't notice the car tailing her two car-lengths back. It took a couple of trips up and down the rows in the parking lot before she found a spot. She quickened her steps across the blacktop to the front steps and hastened up the stairs. Up the elevator to the meeting room, she found the place packed, and her favorite chair already occupied.

Damn.

She looked around until she spotted the couch at the back had room for one more. She dropped her purse on the couch to hold her place and joined the people at the coffee bar. Conversations populated the room in clusters as people discussed how much they had enjoyed the book, many doubting that a movie could do it justice.

The elevator doors opened, and Hewey stepped out along with four others. This was not what he expected. He found a folding chair, one of the last seats available off to the side, scanned the crowd looking for Claire. He spotted her chatting up some man with a ponytail, who was young enough to be their son. He watched her talking, laughing, a smile on her face and found himself wondering why they didn't have conversations like that anymore.

This was why she was always at the library, he thought.

He watched, a sinking feeling in his gut, as the young man lightly touched Claire's arm, before walking over to the giant television.

"Good evening. We have a good crowd for our showing of *The Shawshank Redemption*. If everyone could find a seat, we'll get started. We should have enough chairs, and if not, I can grab a few more folding chairs from downstairs."

When Claire turned, Hewey turned his back and pretended to be looking at the bookshelf behind him. Peeking over his shoulder, he watched her take the corner seat on a couch next to another woman she seemed to know.

"Before I lower the lights, let's do a little quiz. By a show of hands, how many people loved the book?"

Hands shot up from almost everyone, including Claire's.

"Okay. Great. Now. Raise your hand if you think the movie will be as good or better than the book?"

Only a few hands went up this time.

"Interesting. After the movie, we'll ask that question again, then have our discussion. And without further ado, I give you *The Shawshank Redemption*."

Further ado … pretentious little prick, Hewey thought.

Hewey had never seen the movie and assumed he'd sneak out after it started but forgot his plan as he was drawn in by the opening scenes—Andy Dufresne, played by a young Tim Robbins, sits in a darkened car, outside a house, loading bullets into a gun as he drinks bourbon from a bottle. Intercut with the shots from inside the car are courtroom scenes where Andy is on trial for the murder of his wife and her lover and sentenced to two consecutive life sentences.

Hewey was hooked.

Two hours, twenty-two minutes later, Hewey remembers where he is and heads to the elevator while people are still clapping and the lights come on. The elevator opens as he hears the young man with the ponytail ask, "Raise your hand if you think the movie was as good or better than the book?"

Before the door slides closed, he watches as almost every hand in the room is lifted into the air.

***

Claire doesn't come home for another hour. Normally, Hewey would have been zoned out in front of the TV or already asleep, but tonight Claire finds him sitting up waiting for her.

"You're still up," she comments, not expecting much of an answer.

"I'm waiting for you. It's late. Where have you been?" He wants to catch her in a lie, then accuse her of having an affair, even though he knows that isn't true.

"I was at the library."

"Really. Until ten at night?" he pushes.

"It was a special event ... The Book vs The Movie ... We watched *The Shawshank Redemption*. This time the movie won. Any other questions ... detective?" When he didn't say anything else, she started toward the stairs. "I'm going to bed."

"Wait."

She turned. He had an odd expression on his face. "I'm sorry."

That got her attention. "Sorry for what?"

"I'm not quite sure, but I'm picking up on the fact that you aren't happy with me. You moved out of our bathroom. You aren't doing my laundry—"

"I am, if it's in the hamper."

He continued. "You make sure you are gone every night—"

"I'm home Monday and Thursday, and Saturday and Sunday," she countered.

"Right and I'm gone on Monday and Thursday, so basically, we share Saturday and Sunday nights, and this movie thing was on a Saturday, so not even that. I get the feeling you are avoiding me."

A dozen snarky comments flashed across the neural circuits of her cerebral cortex ... Ya think? How does it feel being ignored? I'm surprised you even noticed. Instead, she held her tongue and waited for him to continue.

"Tell me what's wrong," he asked.

She couldn't help herself. "How long do you have?"

"It's that bad?" he asked and looked genuinely surprised.

Of course, he did. He had never taken her complaints seriously. He probably couldn't name a single issue that bothered her, even though they'd had arguments over the course of their marriage about the same things again and again.

"Look. It's late. I'm tired. You're tired. I can make you a list in the morning," she said, and turned to head up the stairs.

"A list!" he blurted out. "I thought this was about dirty underwear on the floor. There's more."

Was he really this clueless after forty years? "There's more. So much more or more accurately, it's about less, not enough of, a lacking."

She watched him put his face in his hands before climbing the stairs. She decided to sleep in the guest room that night.

***

A month later, Hewey and Claire rode the elevator up to the reading room, talking about the movie they were about to see, *Hidden Figures*, based on the novel by Margot Lee Shetterly. While things weren't perfect, Claire had to admit they were better. Hewey had given up one night of bowling and Claire gave up one night at the library. Hewey joined The Book vs The Movie group, and during their evenings at home, they alternated picking what they would watch. Claire didn't move back into their bathroom, enjoying the extra space. Hewey still left towels and clothing on the floor and occasionally ran out of underwear and clean towels and had to run a separate load on his own.

Slowly, over time, many of the little cuts healed. It wasn't perfect, but it was better, and Claire could live with that.

Ω

KILLING TIME

Dressed for success, Kimberly pulled into a Starbucks parking lot and backed into a spot so that she faced the entrance. That morning, she had calculated the amount of time it would take to drive to her interview and had included an additional 45 minutes for traffic, of which there had been none. Now she was early.

Finding the coffee shop a block from where she would be interviewing, she imagined buying a coffee and sitting inside checking emails and her Instagram account. However, when she entered the store she discovered it wasn't a typical Starbucks. There were no clusters of couches, no groupings of chairs around tables, not even a single stool.

Guess they don't want you sticking around, she thought as she paid for her caramel macchiato before returning to her car.

Kimberly checked her email—no offers from her other job interviews; her voicemail—ditto on the "no offers." Checking her social media had her smiling at a couple of cat videos. She didn't click on any of the headlines—she didn't need to be reminded of the "Breaking News" happening every day. Doom and gloom served with your morning coffee. No thank you. She had enough doom and gloom of her own.

The sound of a blaring horn made her look up from her phone. A rusty red pickup truck came inches away from backing into a small blue Honda that was backing out of the opposite parking spot at the same time. Kimberly watched as the two drivers sat, stalemated, until the Honda relented, moving back to let the truck leave.

Moments later, a white BMW with a paper license plate pulled into the spot vacated by the Honda. The car door flew open, and a young woman sprang out, phone in hand, wearing a pink velvet jogging suit that was never meant for jogging. She walked briskly to the entrance, her blonde ponytail bouncing with every step. Seconds later, she returned, coffee in hand, and climbed back into her new car and drove away.

As Kimberly watched this same scenario play out over and over again, she made up stories about the people she watched.

Ponytail girl, with her brand-new BMW, obviously a gift from Daddy, was off to a Pilates class before having lunch at the club with her girlfriends. The only thing Kimberly's daddy had ever given her was herpes.

A couple with the tawny chihuahua had to be newly dating, Kimberly thought, as she watched the boyfriend quicken his steps to open the door for his girlfriend. When was the last time a man had opened a door for her, Kimberly wondered and couldn't think of a single time.

A van pulled up and the sliding door opened. Six young college-aged women in matching sports uniforms climbed out. Based on their height and the time of year, Kimberly guessed they were basketball players here to tank up on caffeine before the big game. While not tall enough to play basketball or volleyball, Kimberly had discovered swimming—with its before and after school practices—to be an excellent excuse to leave home early and come home late, making sure she was never home at the same time as her father, who worked the graveyard shift at Amazon.

She contemplated putting a nasty note on the windshield of the car of a woman who parked in the handicap spot, because she didn't have a blue placard, or a license sticker, or any indication that she was disabled.

"I guess the rules don't apply to you," Kimberly snarked, as she watched the woman hop into her car.

Kimberly's attention turned to a mother struggling to keep her two children in line as the rambunctious boy—who looked to be about five—poked his older sister in the back. An only child, Kimberly wished she'd had a brother, even if he did poke her once in a while. Returning to the car, the mom held her son's hand, her coffee in the other. At the car, she placed the coffee on the roof, before leaning into the back seat to buckle the kids in. Then she climbed into the driver's seat.

Oh, no. Your coffee!

She watched as the mom eased out of the parking spot, turned the wheel, and slowly drove past. Kimberly honked her horn and pointed up, but the woman only looked at her, confusion on her face. Kimberly leaned forward to watch the woman drive away, the coffee cup still balanced on the roof.

Checking the time, she discovered she still had twenty minutes to kill before her interview. This would be her fifth interview this month. Kimberly wasn't hopeful. Her resume told the story of a young woman with a bachelor's degree in Political Science from Cal State Fullerton, that had worked as a paralegal for five years before quitting three weeks ago. When asked why she'd quit, she struggled with finding the politically correct way to say, "My boss was sexually harassing me. Standing too close, touching my hair, and making sexually charged comments when no one was around. I filed a complaint with HR, but they did nothing."

In the first interview, that's exactly what she told the interviewer. The smile froze on the man's face, his eyes grew wide, and his eyebrows sprang up like a pair of McDonald's golden arches as he stuttered, "That's awful."

At the next interview, she tried the same verbiage she'd used when filing for divorce, *irreconcilable differences*. That went over like a fart in an elevator. She watched as the male interviewer scribbled notes on a pad. She imagined him writing, "troublemaker."

During interviews three and four, she'd skirted the real reason for leaving saying she was looking for a position with better opportunities for advancement. That had gotten her exactly nowhere. Everyone says that, she thought.

While she contemplated what she would say in today's interview, she watched a girl, who didn't look old enough to be driving, make several attempts at pulling into the parking spot directly in front of Kimberly's car. The young girl rushed into the coffee shop and returned moments later, coffee in hand. Reverse lights came on, as the kid backed up on a collision course with Kimberly's front fender.

Kimberly blasted her horn, and the girl stopped, looking in her rear-view mirror for the first time. It took four attempts of pulling forward, backing up, pulling forward, and backing up until the driver finally realized she needed to turn the wheel *before* she was completely out of the space.

A lull in the morning rush of coffee addicts brought sparrows out of the trees to pick at crumbs scattered on the ground from crumbly breakfast muffins. During the brief moment of silence, Kimberly heard a deep melodious voice singing. Turning in her seat, Kimberly found the source of the song. A man slowly made his way through the parking lot, each step taken with care as if he were stepping on sharp rocks. He was a symphony in brown—dirty coffee-colored pants held up with a leather belt, old dirt brown boots that scuffed the asphalt with every step, a heavy jacket that reminded Kimberly of a Russet potato complete with dirt stains, and a chestnut brown beanie pulled down over his caramel brown skull. He carried a wrinkled paper bag in one hand and a pink aluminum baseball bat in the other—the only thing not some shade of brown. Once in front of the coffee shop, he settled himself onto the low wall of the planter.

Kimberly wouldn't have given the man a second look, labeling him a crazy homeless person, except for his voice. His voice was rich and flavorful like the coffee he hoped to earn with his performance.

Kimberly rolled down her windows. The melody wasn't something she recognized but it was upbeat, with a jazzy flare that reminded her of one special date to a nightclub with a premed student who thought that by going to jazz clubs and mingling with the local crowd their "coolness" would rub off on him. It didn't.

Checking the time once more before leaving her car, Kimberly approached the man, stopping several feet away as he lit up a cigarette. Seeing her, the man turned, a wide smile revealing several missing teeth.

"Good morning, Sunshine. How you doin' on this fine day?"

"Better because of your singing. What was that song?" Kimberly asked, stepping closer until a wall of odor—part cigarette smoke, part body odor, part something else—stopped her.

"Why that old thang. It's just a little ditty I made up. I call it my walking song. I sing it as I walk. Keeps my mind off my sore feet." He lifted a foot to show her the bottom of his boot.

Kimberly could see newspaper through a large hole in the sole of the shoe and assumed there would be a matching hole in the other shoe. "I think you have a beautiful voice. Were you a professional singer?"

"Sang in the choir back in the day. Now I sing for my supper," he winked, his milk chocolate brown eyes twinkling.

Kimberly knew he expected her to hand him a dollar or something, but she'd left her purse in the car. "Sing me your favorite song," she asked.

Like putting a coin in a jukebox, the man tilted back his head, closed his eyes, and began singing a version of the song *Summertime* that would have given Ella Fitzgerald and Louis Armstrong a run for their money. His dulcet tones gathered a small crowd like the Pied Piper gathered rats and had people pausing to listen. Kimberly used the moment to slip back to her car where she took a twenty from her wallet and returned in time to hear him sing about hushing the baby, telling it not to cry.

He didn't have a hat or an open guitar case, so Kimberly had to step in close to hand him the folded bill. When he saw the denomination, his eyes lit up and he pushed himself to a stand.

"Thank you, beautiful. Can I give you a hug?"

Not wanting to insult the man, she stepped into his outstretched arms. Even though the odor was overpowering, his hug was not. It was warm and sincere. He embraced her, saying, "Thank you, thank you." When he released her, she stepped back, a bit shaken. That hug had been the most genuine sign of affection she'd received in years.

"Listen to me now," he said, his voice warm like melted butter. "Today is going to be a good day for you. You're a good, honest person. Remember that, okay?"

Kimberly looked into the man's smiling face and wondered how he could be so happy living as he did, while even though she had an apartment, a running car, and enough money to put food on her plate, most days she had to talk herself into getting out of bed and smiling... What was there to smile about?

As she walked back to her car, the man launched into the Beatles' song *Good Day Sunshine*, the melody sticking with her like the slight smell of cigarette smoke and BO. As she exited the parking lot, she kept her windows open and cranked the air conditioning to dispel any lingering odor that may have rubbed off on her.

***

For the first time, the person interviewing her was a woman. When it came time to answer the inevitable question of why she quit her last job, she started by saying, "I'm looking for a position with better opportunities."

The woman, dressed in an immaculate blue suit and crisp white blouse, looked bored, as she wrote notes on a pad. Then Kimberly remembered the words of the homeless man, "You're a good and honest person." Why was she ashamed to say what really happened? She hadn't done anything wrong. She decided right there and then, to tell the truth, and if this company didn't like it or thought she was a troublemaker, then why would she want to work for them anyway?

Kimberly cleared her throat and sat up taller. "While it's true, I do want a position with a path for advancement, better pay, and benefits, that is not the reason I left my previous job."

The woman paused, her pen hung over the page and she looked up. Kimberly had her attention now.

Two days later, the phone rang. The company made her an offer, one that included healthcare and a matching retirement plan. Turns out, the woman who interviewed her had experienced a similar situation early in her career and liked how Kimberly had not danced around the subject but had given her an honest answer.

The morning after Kimberly cashed her first paycheck, she sat in the Starbucks parking lot waiting for the singing man. Again, she heard his music before she saw him. She watched as he shuffled over to his spot in the same old shoes and sat on the short wall as he sang a bluesy song that was so beautiful it made her want to cry.

"Hello, beautiful. Happy to see you again," he said when she walked up.

Kimberly set a large bag on the wall next to the man. He leaned toward it and looked inside. Sitting on top of a pile of folded clothing including socks, pants, a long-sleeved thermal shirt, and a plaid flannel shirt, were a pair of boots. She'd bought everything at a local thrift store that sold gently worn clothing.

"Those are some nice shoes there." He picked one up and turned it over. "Look. No hole."

Kimberly nodded. "No holes. I didn't know your exact size, so I guessed and added some socks in case they are too large."

"What's your name, beautiful?"

"Kimberly."

"I'm Benjamin, but my friends call me Bennie. Let me sing you a song, Kimberly, to start your day off right."

CALLISTO

As I approach the restaurant, I remove my health monitor from my wrist and tuck it into my purse. Tonight, I'm going to drink and eat whatever sounds good. The last thing I need is an incessant beeping warning me I'm off my plan. I'm celebrating!

At the door, posted bold and proud, is a large triple-A sign – a triple A rating is the best air quality possible.

Trish went all out for this, I think, as I reach for the handle.

Once through the double-door airlock, I remove my ventilator before following the hostess to join my friends. Upon seeing me, a shout goes out, "She's here!" All eyes turn to me.

Several people rush to greet me. I return their hugs and cheek kisses with equal enthusiasm. Trish hooks my arm with hers and leads me to my place of honor, the head of the table. That's when I see the banner.

Happy Embryo Transfer Day!

"Oh my God. Who came up with that?" I'm undecided whether to be mortified or thrilled.

Lionel raises his hand, a pleased smile on his face. "It was Trish's idea, but I added the swimming sperm."

Looking more closely, I make out what appears to be little tadpoles all swimming towards what I assume is an egg.

Turning to Lionel, my cheeks flush pink. "You know that's not what is going on here. It's all done in a petri dish. Then the fertilized egg is transferred," I tell him, keeping my voice steady and the information clinical.

Lionel shrugs. "My way is more romantic."

Of course, Lionel would think that. Most guys do. They want to keep trying again and again. "It's all about enjoying the process," he'd said after our fifth attempt at making a baby.

For me, while the "process" was okay, it was the results that mattered, especially since my biological clock continued its relentless countdown. In another year, I'll be forty and officially disqualified from any breeding assistance. Between population control restrictions (one child per person) and health code regulations (DNA testing for inheritable diseases) I needed to stop dicking around—literally and figuratively.

Like most women of the twenty-fifth century, I opted for The Vault, the worldwide sperm bank where each donor had their DNA and IQ tested. I found the selection process fascinating. Using filters—ethnicity, eye color, height, hair color, hair type, and so much more—I narrowed down the field. With one click, the system combined my genetic features with my selected donor's features, creating probable outcomes for a girl and a boy. It then presented me with 3D models of each child at ages three, seven, eleven, fifteen, and nineteen Including the disclaimer: "Results may vary." Duh.

Dozens of matches later, I found the guy … Donor 275632. Tall (5'11" – two inches taller than me), athletic build (passed all the cardio and physical tests) thick, wavy brown hair (that will hopefully counteract my thin, straight chestnut mane), and deep blue eyes, the color of the pre-war ocean (My eyes are chocolate brown but include a recessive blue gene giving me a chance at a blue-eyed baby.) I'd left the ethnicity box unchecked, not concerned about skin tones and casting a larger net.

Donor 275632 hails from what used to be Italy before all the country lines were blurred and half the population fled off planet, leaving the rest of us behind.

I purposely picked a donor that had died years ago, to eliminate the possibility of randomly running into the guy, or my child doing a search for their biological. Don't need *that* kind of drama.

Trish takes her champagne flute, lifting it high. "To baby 275632-A and his or her fabulous mother."

"I'll drink to that."

***

Baby 275632-A had stopped being a number to me the first time I felt movement. Then, when I found out I was carrying a boy, I named him, Callisto, after one of Jupiter's moons. His friends can call him Cal for short.

Ripe and ready to burst at the seams, I have my feet up and my eyes closed, imagining my life as a mother… watching my sweet baby boy sleep, encouraging his first steps, placing a sterile strip on a scrapped knee, cheering him on as he plays soccer under the park dome. In my mind, I'm cheering and clapping for my little man, when I feel a gush of warm water wash down my legs.

This is it. Before I have a chance to stand up, my health monitor signals an incoming call.

"Hello."

"According to our data, your water just broke. Is that correct?"

"Yes. I was just about to call you."

"No need. We are sending a car. Be ready in fifteen minutes," the very efficient voice instructed.

Not a person, I think, or there would have been a hint of excitement, an encouraging statement.

I text Trish before standing. "It's D-Day!"

In the bathroom, I fold a towel and place it between my legs. The first contraction hits as I brush my teeth. If my water hadn't broken, I probably would have ignored such a weak spasm. When the flow of amniotic fluid slows to a drip, I change my clothes, securing a pad in place. My suitcase has been packed for weeks so there isn't much to do except grab my stuff and head downstairs to the lobby. Right on time, the transport pulls in front of the building. I watch the ventilator-wearing driver stretch the accordion tunnel from the transport to the entrance of the building so I can walk ventilator-free to the waiting vehicle. I feel like a celebrity.

***

The contractions come fast and hard. Months of classes didn't prepare me for this. My nurse, Agnes, has kind hazel eyes, which is the only feature I can see since a cap and mask cover the rest of her face. She wipes my forehead. "You're almost there. Keep breathing."

A piercing alarm echoes off the walls of the delivery room.

"What's that?"

Agnes checks the baby monitor. "No. No, no, no. Not again."

The distress in Agnes's voice blankets me with a feeling of dread and has my heart racing. What does she mean by, "Not Again."

"What's happening?"

Before she can explain, a masked doctor and another nurse enter the room, take one look at the monitor, and announce, "The baby is in distress. We need to do an emergency C-section. Nurse. Call the OR."

Agnes is frozen in place, staring at the monitor.

"Nurse!"

Agnes turns, looks directly at me. Her eyes look so sad. A tear glistens. As she reaches to take my hand, the other nurse, tall and lean, pushes between us saying in a harsh voice, "Go." Before lifting the side rails of my bed and unlocking the wheels.

Bright, harsh lights have me closing my eyes. The contractions are still coming. There is a bustle of activity.

"This can't be happening. No, no, no. Please, save my baby," I manage to say before my nose and mouth are covered and I'm instructed to breathe normally. I open my eyes only to watch the light fade into darkness.

***

I'm swimming up, up, up, through an inky blackness to a ripple of light above. I work to open my eyes, my eyelids heavy and uncooperative. Eyes finally open, an unfamiliar ceiling stares down at me. It takes a moment to remember where I am and what has happened. I reach for my stomach with both hands. The hard mound is deflated into a soft wobbly pancake. My baby.

I look around the room. There is no clear hospital bassinet, only stark white walls and a monitor beeping rhythmically.

"Hello." My voice is weak and scratchy.

Searching, I locate a call button. Within moments, a nurse appears. "Yes. Do you need something?"

"My baby. I need my baby."

The nurse shakes her head. "I'm sorry. Your baby didn't survive. The umbilical cord was wrapped around his throat. We did everything we could. I'm so sorry." Her voice is soft and kind, but her eyes are cold.

"Can I get you something for the pain?"

I'm confused. Is there something you can take to erase the pain of losing your baby? Before I realize it, an anguished wail escapes my lips, sounding like a wild animal caught in a trap. I move to sit up. I must escape this place, this fate. That's when the physical pain hits me.

The nurse gently pushes me down. "You need to calm yourself. Your cries will disturb the other mothers on this floor. You've had a C-Section. You need to rest. We'll be sending you home in a couple of days. I'll get you some pain meds."

When the nurse leaves, I pull the pillow from under my head and press it to my face. I scream and scream and scream until my throat is raw.

***

I've been home for two days now after spending three days in the hospital. Work has given me another week off to "get over my loss." If I'd had the baby, I would have received six months of maternity leave … but no baby, no leave. Trish came over the first day I was home and stayed the night. We drank wine and cried, then drank more wine and cried some more. Trish must have said, "I'm soooo sorry" dozens of times before I told her to stop. She wanted to stay longer but she'd used all her personal days and had to return to work.

A postpartum nurse is due to arrive shortly to "counsel" me. Unless she brings my little Callisto, I don't know what she can do. This grief is a physical weight pressing down on me, making it difficult to breathe, get out of bed, walk across the room. I wish my Mom were still alive. She lived through three miscarriages before she had me. She would understand my pain in a way Trish or some random nurse cannot.

My security camera alerts me that someone is coming up the stairs. A hooded person, short in stature, wearing a respirator, approaches my door. While my apartment has a B+ air rating, our apartment corridors are only C-. The owner justifies this explaining, "Why spend money purifying spaces that aren't lived in."

Two gentle knocks. I open the door and look into familiar hazel eyes... Agnes. I motion her inside. She removes her ventilator and slides the black hood from her head revealing a curly mass of gray hair. I had no idea she was so old. She steps forward and embraces me in a hug. She pushes up on tiptoes until her warm breath tickles the hairs near my ear. "They are listening. Don't react."

I pull out of her embrace, confusion furrowing my brow. I open my mouth to speak. She shakes her head and puts a finger to her lips.

"My name is Agnes. I will be your post-partum nurse. May I have a seat?"

I nod and gesture to the sofa. "Can I get you something? I have UV purified water. I could make tea."

Agnes smiles and nods, giving me a thumbs up. "I'm good. Thank you. The real question is how are you?"

I shrug. I'm not sure what I'm supposed to say. Who is listening? What is going on here?

"It's okay if you are sad. That's very natural." Agnes pulls a three-ring binder from her bag and hands it to me, pantomiming that I should open the binder. She points at the words on the first page.

I read. *We will be having two conversations. The verbal conversation is for those listening. The other conversation is written out. If you wish to continue, nod. Now say, "I am a bit sad," then turn the page.*

"I am sad. I lost my baby. It's a difficult time."

"Yes, I know. I'm here to help you." Agnes smiles and nods as I turn the page.

What I'm about to tell you is shocking. You mustn't react. If you do, I will make up something to cover your reaction. If you are ready to learn the truth about your baby, take a deep breath and turn the page.

What could this possibly be about? My hands tremble as I turn the page.

YOUR BABY IS ALIVE.

I can't help it. I grasp.

"Now, now. Please don't cry. I know this is difficult."

Agnes keeps talking while I take a minute to compose myself. I sniff a couple of times to sell the idea that I'm crying.

"Here's a tissue," Agnes offers, although her hand is empty. She points to the book and motions for me to turn the page.

I'm going to keep talking and "comforting" you, while you continue to read. Remember, don't say anything.

I look up. Agnes points to the book and starts talking. "Post-partum depression is a real thing, even for women who deliver a healthy baby. So, it's only natural that you would be depressed. I'm here to help you. Your insurance plan provides for three visits … "

Agnes's voice drones on about I don't know what, as my mind tries to comprehend what I'm reading.

Yes, you read that correctly. Your baby is alive and well. You did not need an emergency C-section. The baby was not distressed. What you saw on the monitor was pre-recorded and patched in … everything planned from the day you applied for IVF. You were on a watch list. You checked all the boxes … no husband/boyfriend, no parents, no siblings, few friends, no genetic diseases, no addictions, pleasant features, and above-average IQ.

I look up to see Agnes watching me intently, a finger to her lips, even as she keeps up the one-sided conversation. She points to the book and indicates that I should keep reading.

There is a group of people, people with money, lots of money, who, for whatever reason, can no longer have children. So, they steal them, steal them from women like you who have no support, no money, and no means to question or investigate what has happened. They are very good at what they do. They have friends in all the right places … the hospitals, the police, the politicians.

The good news is there is another network of people who attempt to steal these babies back for the rightful mother. We have a 60 percent success rate and we, too, have infiltrated the hospitals, law enforcement, and government, although not high-ranking people ... worker bees like me. If you are interested in learning more, nod your head.

I nod my head so hard I think it might pop off my neck. I reach over and grab Agnes's hand and squeeze it, hoping to convey the strength of my commitment.

Agnes nods. "I have a small supply of anti-depressants I can give you. I will also need to collect your government-issued health monitor. I'll come back tomorrow, if you like, to check up on you and answer any questions you might have."

"Yes, that would be great."

Agnes points to the book, I flip the page to read, *"DO NOT TELL ANYONE. ANYONE! IF YOU DO, YOU'LL NEVER SEE YOUR CHILD OR ME AGAIN. THEY ARE LISTENING BUT SO ARE WE. This is going to happen quickly for the sake of you and the child, but some sacrifices must be made, sacrifices that once set in motion cannot be undone. Nod if you understand.*

I mouth the words, "I understand," even though I don't. At this point, I will agree to anything if it means seeing my baby and holding him in my arms.

Agnes stands. "Okay. Does the same time tomorrow work for you?"

"Yes. That would be fine. I appreciate you coming."

Agnes motions for me to flip one more page. I do and read. *Open the binder and pull out these pages. Take them into the bathroom after I leave, rip them into tiny pieces, and flush them. There can be no traces of our conversation, for all of our sake. No phone calls, texts, emails. I'm your contact and I will meet with you two more times. I'll explain everything.*

"Let me walk you to the door."

"That won't be necessary. I can let myself out. You rest up now. Put on some calming music and relax. I'll see you tomorrow."

In the bathroom, door closed, sitting on the edge of the bathtub, I can hear the music from the living room. I re-read each page, especially the page that says *my baby is alive*, before tearing the sheets into pieces the size of my thumb. Unanswered questions race inside my head… Who are "they"? How can they get away with this? Who is the network? What sacrifice will I be asked to make?

As I flush the last of the pages, I feel something new … hope. And more importantly, determination.

***

At the end of Agnes's third and final visit, she gave me a fierce hug and whispered, "Good luck," before walking out the door, never to be seen by me again.

Today, I'm disappearing from the world. I feel bad for Trish, the only person on the planet who will care that I've died. My instructions are simple. Write a letter, a suicide note, and leave it in the apartment along with everything I own … phone, purse, respirator. I'm to pack no bag. New clothing will be provided. During her last visit, Agnes left me a mini respirator to use for my journey. I'm to wear a heavy coat with a hoodie underneath. I've been given a route to follow through the park to the river. At a specific location where there are no cameras, I'm to toss my coat and shoes into the water. Another woman will meet me, with a different-looking coat, scarf, and hat, plus a new pair of boots. Arm in arm, we will walk out of the park to a waiting van. Agnes told me if I follow their instructions, this will work. Do not deviate from the plan. Have faith, she told me.

Opening the door, I stop and look back at my apartment. It's not much but it was mine. The credits I had saved for my son's future have been donated to various charities, all of which are fronts for the community where I will be living … living with my son. The thought fills me with joy.

A small voice, my father's no doubt, puts my fears into words. *This is all a scam. They've taken all your money and now they will take your life. You've made it easy for them, even writing the suicide note. No one will look for you. No one will question that you killed yourself. You were always so weak.*

No. I saw the picture. My baby is alive.

How do you know that was your baby? It could be any baby. You're such a fool.

Well, at least I'm willing to sacrifice everything for my child, which is more than you ever did for me. And with that, I close the door on my former life.

***

Slowly I regain consciousness. Muted voices and strangely enough, birds singing, coax me awake. My first thought … this must be a dream. Then I remember where I'm supposed to be and what I have done… no, it's a nightmare.

I remember climbing into a van, fastening my safety belt and harness, and then a hand reaching around from behind, covering my mouth and nose with a damp, sweet-smelling cloth. I was drugged.

I force my eyes open to find I'm in a hospital bed, but unlike the hospital where I had my C-section, the walls are painted a sunny yellow, and a huge picture window frames a large tree, where several blackbirds take turns chirping. Birds outside. How odd. I push myself up, the effort making me gasp in pain.

A door opens. I woman about my age enters. "I'm Claire. I know you must be scared, confused, even angry. I know I was, but I know someone who will make it all better."

Claire walks to the corner of the room to a bassinet I hadn't noticed. Carefully she lifts a small bundle. "Would you like to meet your son?"

I have no words. Tears cloud my vision as I stretch out my arms. Claire places a sleeping child in my arms. A living, breathing angel. Cradled in the crook of my arm, pressed against my chest, I bend my head until our noses touch. I inhale deeply his sweet smell. A tear lands on his forehead. He flinches. Arching his back, his forehead wrinkles, his mouth opens making a perfect little O. When he opens his eyes, I stare into a pair of indigo eyes.

"He has blue eyes," I say in wonder.

Claire steps back. "He's going to be hungry soon. He's a good eater. Really latches on. But let me know if you need help. Let him cry a bit. It will help trigger your milk."

I barely notice when Claire leaves. I only have eyes for Callisto.

***

Callisto and I live in a small cottage that is part of a circle of small cottages with a fountain and grass in the middle. The dome overhead means we can move about freely without respirators. The outside world thinks this is a colony for the diseased … people infected and contagious. It used to be, but those people died and the nurses and workers who lived here, secretly repurposed the place.

To keep the outside world away, news stories of The Terrible Sickness, in all its gory details, are released to the press and social media. No one would willingly come here and that is just the way we want it.

We will live here until Cal is ready to enter first grade. Then we will emerge from our domed chrysalis like a butterfly from the past, with new identities, fresh opportunities. We have options as to where to put down roots, even off planet. Once safe, we will start again, My baby boy and me.

SUMMER

Playmates, neighbors, friends for our entire lives, Joey is "just Joey" as in the answer to the question, "Is that your boyfriend?"

"No. It's just Joey."

Until the sunscreen.

Laying on lounge chairs at Joey's parent's house next to the pool, Joey and I are home from college for the summer. It's not the first time we'd applied sunscreen to each other's backs, but this time it feels different.

Joey's hands move slowly, deliberately, spending extra time applying a slight pressure along the edge of my shoulder blades with his thumbs, his hands saying something, his lips don't dare.

"My turn," I say, holding out my hand for the tube of sunscreen.

Our eyes lock as he hands it over before turning away and presenting his broad muscular back to me. As I lovingly apply the lotion, my hands acknowledge that I've received his message, and I feel the same.

Ω

BEST BIRTHDAY EVER

The last tendrils of sleep float away like cobwebs in a light breeze. Strands of her dream cling stubbornly to Connie's first conscience thoughts.

The beach. She was at the beach. The sensation of warm sand squeezing between her toes, and the shock of the salty cold surf surrounding her ankles made her shiver as the sound of seagulls screeching, circling overhead against a blinding blue sky, echoed inside her head … it had all felt so real.

Connie rubs her feet together, wondering if she'll discover granules of sand stuck between her toes. Finding none, she feels disappointed. Now that she's fully awake, Connie hears the distant roar of the surf hitting sand.

It must be high tide. The waves are closer, louder, at high tide.

Lying in bed, listening to the soothing white noise of water pounding sand, Connie is ready to surrender to the comfort of her bed when it dawns on her … today is her birthday, her 90th birthday. For once, she has a reason to get up. She grabs her glasses and checks the time.

8:30. Still plenty of time.

With care, Connie sits up and swings her legs, one at a time, over the side of the bed. She allows her body time to adjust to the new position. Using her cane for stability, Connie presses down on the edge of the bed with her other hand to push herself to a stand.

Wait. Make sure you are balanced before moving.

After four tentative steps, Connie is at the window where she can hold onto the windowsill for support. Gazing out across the tops of other apartment buildings, Connie sees the glistening of sunlight on water.

So close.

Connie's son, Andrew, will be arriving at 11 to take her to a local restaurant where her family will gather for her birthday lunch. She was against the idea from the start. A long table filled with her four children, their spouses, nine grandchildren, and one great-grandchild, with Connie seated at the head of the table.

"I won't be able to hear a thing," she'd protested. "The noise of so many people talking in a confined space sounds like the buzzing of a hundred bees."

"Everyone will come up to you to talk," Bridget, her daughter-in-law and the planner of the event, had explained.

"I'm not a queen. I don't want to be at the head of the table."

"Fine," Bridget sighed, letting her frustration with Connie drip through like a leaking faucet.

"It's not how I want to celebrate," Connie had tried.

"How *do* you want to celebrate?"

"I would—"

Bridget didn't let her continue. "We are not going to let you sit home alone on your 90th birthday. Everyone is coming. It will be great. You'll see," was Bridget's final argument.

Connie had let it go. The reservation had been made. Airline tickets purchased. Hotels booked. The good thing would be to have everyone together. But she was still convinced that sitting in a restaurant was *not* going to be a good thing.

As Connie goes through her morning routine-- bathroom, coffee, bathroom again, dress, then out on the tiny balcony with a second cup of coffee and her favorite chocolate and caramel biscotti—a feeling of dread works its way into her bones like the arthritis that makes it difficult to walk. She can't stop thinking about the gathering at the restaurant.

The grandkids will be bored out of their minds. The parents will spend more time making sure the kids are behaving, especially that little sneak Tommy, than enjoying themselves. Take your eyes off that one and you could find him taking bread from some other table's basket.

Even though Tommy was a rascal of the first order, his shenanigans made Connie smile especially since he was Brad's son. Brad had been a handful and Connie remembered telling him as a teenager—after he was caught jumping from their roof to their neighbor's—that she hoped he had a son just like him. And he had.

It's not going to be fun for anyone, especially me.

Months ago, when Bridget had asked her what she wanted to do for her 90th she hadn't had an answer, but now she did. It came to her as vividly as her dream. She wanted to go to the beach. She picks up her phone and calls her son.

"I don't want to go to the restaurant."

With a laugh, Andrew shoots back, "Well good morning to you too, and happy birthday."

"Yes, yes. Good morning. Now listen. I've given this a lot of thought …" *Which I haven't, but he won't know that.* "The restaurant will be too noisy, and the grandkids will be bored or on their phones and tablets the whole time. I don't want to have my 90th birthday party at a stuffy old restaurant."

"But it's your birthday, we want to celebrate with you, celebrate YOU. Everyone is coming. It's all been arranged. You can't sit there alone on your birthday," Andrew tries.

"Who said anything about sitting here alone? I want to celebrate with the family, just not at a restaurant."

I'm not backing down this time. After all, it's my birthday. We should do what I want to do, for once.

"So … what *do* you want to do?"

"I want to go to the beach." Connie smiles as she imagines the shock on Andrew's face.

"The beach?"

"Yes. The beach. You know. That place where the sand meets the ocean."

"Ninety years old and still a smartass," Andrew teases.

"It's a beautiful day. That restaurant Bridget picked is a block from the beach. Call and cancel the reservation, grab beach towels, chairs, sunscreen, and pack a lunch. We're going to the beach."

"But Mom, Bridget is going to lose her mind. She has decorations. A cake. We will forfeit our deposit for canceling such a large party at the last minute," Andrew argues.

"Bring the cake, bring the decorations, tell the restaurant the guest of honor died."

"Jesus, Mom. That's not funny."

"It's kind of funny," Connie tries. *Andrew has always been the sensitive one.* "Don't worry. I'm feeling fine. I just want to go to the beach. Put my toes in the sand one more time. Think of it as my dying wish."

"Oh, dear god. A guilt trip? Really?"

Connie giggles. "Whatever it takes. Don't worry. I'll pay the restaurant fee. Now get on the phone and call everyone. Tell them to pack their lunches and bring their beach stuff. And tell Bridget thank you for planning my party. I really appreciate all the work that went into getting everyone to come out."

"This is really what you want?" Andrew asks.

"Yes. The grandkids are going to love this and so am I. I gotta go. I need to make my sandwich. Tell Bridget I'm looking forward to the cake. Love you," she says in a sing-song voice.

She can hear her son's sigh. "Love you back."

Connie spends the next hour making peanut butter and jelly sandwiches and deciding what to wear. She texts her boys to remind them to bring shovels and sand toys. She is looking forward to building a sandcastle.

Apparently, Andrew survived the wrath of Bridget since he arrives at her door with a smile on his face.

"You were right. The kids are thrilled," he says as he picks up her beach bag.

"And Bridget?"

Andrew shrugs. "It was a hard sell, but my charm and good looks won her over in the end … that and you offering to pay the restaurant fee."

"Always on a budget, that one," Connie says not unkindly.

"It's why we're not broke. Let's go. We are meeting everyone at Lifeguard Station number 3."

***

Everyone admits it's a perfect beach day, a rare phenomenon for a Saturday in June in Southern California … clear blue sky, a light breeze, small waves for the kids, and not too crowded. Getting Connie down by the water is a challenge. The grandkids race to the water's edge, shedding clothes and shoes faster than fall leaves being ripped from trees in a hurricane, all before Connie has walked ten feet across the uneven sand. Cane in one hand, a death grip on her daughter-in-law Keri's arm with the other, they make slow progress heading toward the water.

Her two sons hurry past, carrying an ice chest, a box of food, and several umbrellas tucked under their arms. By the time they dump everything and return to help, Connie has made it another ten feet and puffing with exhaustion.

"I got you, Mom," says Brad the younger brother as he hooks his arm under Connie's knees and lifts her up. "Put your hands around my neck."

"Ohhhh," Connie squeals. "I haven't been carried like this since your father carried me across the threshold."

"Show off," says Andrew, before heading back to the parking lot for another load.

"Where do you want to sit," Brad asks as he marches across the sand as if Connie weighs next to nothing, his wife following with Connie's cane.

"Down by the water. It's the best spot for building sandcastles. You did bring sand toys, didn't you?"

"We did," says Keri. "We had to dig through boxes in the garage. It's been years since the kids have played with them since discovering boogie boarding."

Moments later, Brad lowers Connie to the sand. "How's this?"

Connie inhales the thick salty air, digs her fingers into the warm sand, and watches as a wave inches its way toward her. "Perfect. Just perfect."

Sand toys arrive followed by two of the younger grandkids. "You know how to make a sandcastle, right?" she asks.

They shake their heads in unison.

These grandkids—Molly, seven, and Tyler, five—belong to her daughter Theresa and her husband Rick who live in Las Vegas, Nevada. Plenty of sand, even a knight's castle, but no sandcastles.

"We need water. Who wants to take a bucket and collect water?"

Both Molly and Tyler's hands shoot up.

Connie hands them each a bucket. "Off you go. Try not to spill it all on your way back," she calls out to their backsides as they dash away.

While the kids walk back so carefully that Connie wonders if she'll still be alive by the time they return, she removes her shoes and socks before digging a hole for her feet. Now she sits upright with her feet in the hole as if she were sitting in a straight-back chair. This is a trick she'd perfected as a young mother with four children and not enough hands to bring a beach chair.

As the castle takes shape, growing larger and more complicated, it attracts the older grandkids like seagulls to a bag of potato chips until everyone is working on the construction project. The older kids create a channel that brings water into the moat with every surge of the wave. Connie shows two of the girls how to make decorative formations that look like drippy stalagmites with a slurry of sand and water. Collected seashells become fancy windows, feathers stand in as flags, and a line of seaweed forms a road leading to a drawbridge made of driftwood.

It doesn't take long for the parents to join them, taking pictures of the amazing creation. A large wave breaches the castle's wall amid shrill screams from the kids and laughter from the adults. The wave fills Connie's hole at her feet, and she shudders with the shock of the chilly Pacific Ocean water. The water quickly soaks in, and Connie wriggles her toes into the wet sand just like in her dream.

Connie takes joy in every moment, feeling, maybe not exactly like a kid again, what with her aching knees and arthritic fingers, but at the very least like the mother she used to be, taking her kids to the beach a dozen times during the summer.

"Lunchtime," Bridget announces, causing the kids to drop their shovels and buckets before dashing up to the blankets and collection of umbrellas.

Brad and Andrew pull Connie to her feet and help her walk back up to the area where a proper lawn chair awaits her. Food is laid out on a pallet covered with a tablecloth, her birthday cake taking a star position in the center. Connie learns they plan on burning the pallet in one of the fire pits before they leave. The kids scarf down Connie's peanut and jelly sandwiches, ignoring the store-bought hoagies, which makes her smile.

Connie isn't hungry. She feels full of happiness, full of joy, full of wonder at the family that surrounds her. After much prompting from her kids, she manages to eat a half of a half of a half of a hoagie claiming she's leaving room for "that beautiful cake," which makes Bridget smile.

The birthday song is sung, and two candles—a 9 and a 0—are blown out by the beach breeze before Connie even inhales. Then it's time for the cards and gifts.

Bridget stands. Everyone quiets. Even the kids know that when Aunt Bridget takes charge they better listen up.

"Mom. We know you told us not to get you anything. That you have everything you need and that being with us was the best present possible. But it's your 90th birthday. I just couldn't imagine not doing something … something special for such a special woman."

Spontaneous cheering erupted. Bridget waits for the furor to die down. "Each family was tasked with getting you 90-somethings."

Connie felt a moment of panic.

Ninety times four families? Where will I put all this stuff?

Seeing the look of panic and confusion on Connie's face she rushed on. "Don't worry. You're not getting 90 toasters or 90 beach towels. It's a 90-themed something. You'll see. Who wants to go first?"

Molly's hand shoots up. "Me. Me. I want to go first." She jumps to her feet and rushes over to her mom who hands her a soft purple drawstring bag that Connie is pretty sure used to hold a bottle of Crown Royal whiskey.

Setting the bag in Connie's lap, Molly demands, "Open it."

Before Connie has even loosened the golden cord holding the bag closed, Molly blurts out, "It's pennies. Ninety pennies. One for each year. Get it. Ninety years old, ninety pennies. Tyler and I collected them. Do you love it?"

"I do. I really do. Thank you," Connie says, pulling Molly into her arms.

Tyler runs up and pushes his way into the embrace. "I helped. I helped."

"Yes, thank you, Tyler. These pennies are just what I wanted," Connie says, smiling over the tops of the kids' heads to mouth the words "Thank You" to Theresa and Rick.

Theresa steps forward. "It's not as exciting as 90 pennies, but you might be able to spend this before your next birthday," she says as she hands Connie a gift card.

"Ninety dollars credit?" Connie asks.

"Yup," says Rick. "And you can use it online if you want, too."

Ever the practical one.

"Thank you all," Connie says as she reluctantly releases Molly and Tyler from her embrace.

And so it goes, gift cards for ninety dollars, a daisy chain made of ninety links, and the gift that got the most oohs and aahs, ninety scratchers, from Bridget and Andrew.

"Can we scratch them off now?" asks Jonathan, one of the older grandkids.

"Sure. What should we use?" Connie wonders out loud.

"The pennies," Molly squeals. "But you have to give the pennies back when you're done, okay?" she says sternly.

For the next ten minutes, everyone has their heads down as they concentrate on scratching off the coating to reveal prizes. Shouts of, "I won a dollar!" "I won five!" punctuates the air. The biggest prize is a fifty-dollar winner won by 14-year-old Daniel who is very disappointed when he learns he doesn't get to keep the money.

"Oh, give it to him," Connie tries but is overruled.

With the scratchers scratched, the kids lose interest and return to the water, leaving the adults in the shade of the umbrellas.

"Was this everything you imagined your birthday party to be?" asks Theresa.

Connie nods. "Everything and more. Thank you all for showing up. It means so much to me." Tears escape the corners of Connie's eyes. "Best birthday ever," she manages to say before she puts her face in her hands and lets the tears flow.

One by one, her kids and their spouses come over and give her a hug, which just makes it worse. More tears slide down her cheeks and drop off her jaw until she's begging for a napkin or something to blow her nose.

Her oldest granddaughter, Monica, a new mother herself, has stayed back with the other adults. "Would you like to hold your great-granddaughter?"

Because she can't speak without her voice cracking, Connie simply holds out her arms. Monica places Carly in her grandmother's arms.

Bending forward, Connie nuzzles her nose into the crook of Carly's neck and inhales deeply. The new baby smell whisks her back in time to that moment when her child was placed in her arms, and she became a mother for the first time.

How can that be 70 years ago? Where has the time gone?

Brad gently pushes Monica and her mom toward Connie, and pulls out his phone. "Four generations of Wallace women. Good job, Mom. Now, wipe your tears and smile."

And she did.

Best birthday ever.

Ω

THE RETRIEVER

It started innocently enough with a bag of Fritos. I'd rolled my wheelchair under the outstretched limbs of a chestnut tree and faced the huge expanse of lawn that is Central Park's Sheep Meadow. Twisting and reaching around, I pulled Reggie's once yellow tennis ball from my satchel. Turning back, Reggie stood at attention, eyes locked on the grimy ball, nose twitching in anticipation.

Cocking my arm, I let the ball fly. Reggie raced off. I'd barely had time to open my book when Reggie returned and dropped the ball onto my thighs. This was our routine. Throw, read, retrieve, drop. After a dozen tosses and retrievals, Reggie brought me something different … an unopened bag of Fritos.

"Where'd you get these?"

Reggie cocked his head at my question but supplied no answer.

While dozens of people occupied the meadow—couples walking, kids playing, people spread out on blankets—I didn't notice anyone looking frantically about for a lost bag of chips.

Reggie placed a paw on my leg, indicating he wanted something … a Frito. Seeing no one coming to retrieve their snack, I ripped open the bag. Since Golden Retrievers were bred to bring back a duck without damaging it, the curls of fried and salted corn chips were unbroken.

"Good Boy."

Frito for me, Frito for Reggie, until the bag was empty. This was my mistake … rewarding the thief with the spoils of his larceny.

***

Two days later, on our way to the park, I sat at a red light at the corner of 9th and 61st. I use a long retractable leash when walking Reggie, allowing him to trot ahead or drop behind to investigate an intriguing smell. Reggie, somewhere behind me at the end of his leash, needed a slight come-along tug when the light turned green. I heard the whirl of the long tether wind back into the handle as I rolled into the crosswalk, Reggie now by my side.

Parked under my favorite tree as I watched a group playing soccer, Reggie surprised me by dropping a foil wrapped burrito in my lap. He sat in front of me expectantly, his tail brushing the grass as it wagged back and forth. I swear, he was grinning.

"What the hell? Where'd you get this?"

Reggie's ears dropped at my harsh tone. I retraced our route in my mind and remembered Rosa Mexicano, a restaurant with outdoor dining at the corner of 9th and 61st. While I waited for the light, Reggie must have snatched a burrito. Since I hadn't heard irate shouts, I guess he'd gotten away with it. I turned the burrito over in my hand and examined it carefully. No signs this was a discarded meal he'd found on the ground. My stomach growled.

Peeling back the foil, I took a tentative bite. Melted cheese, chunks of pork, just the right amount of beans, onions, cilantro, and salsa. Delicious. About halfway through the burrito, I pulled out a large chunk of carnitas and rewarded the thief.

"You were a very bad dog," I said lovingly.

Reggie responded with tail wagging, and a happy bark. I'd created a monster.

Over the course of the summer, Reggie honed his thieving skills. He nicked two apples from the fruit stand on our way home, holding them in his mouth like a couple of tennis balls, an easy feat for a Golden. He absconded with an entire lunch sack that included, to my delight, a canned cocktail. I knew I should put an end to his thievery but as a legless Veteran on a fixed income, the spoils of his labors were often the highlight of my day.

Reggie did get caught once when he dragged an entire picnic basket across the lawn. I'm not sure if it was my lack of legs, my sincere apology, or Reggie's sad eyes that got us off the hook.

***

After a glorious summer of fresh fruit, sandwiches, bags of cookies, and whatever Reggie could find unguarded, our free meals came to a screeching halt, when Reggie carried over a leather attaché case by the handle. I flipped open the double locks to find a wad of cash and a pastrami on rye from Katz's Delicatessen … the tantalizing aroma baiting my dog.

"Oh shit." Looking around I spotted the supposed owner, a man dressed for the financial district not Sheep Meadow, having an animated conversation on his phone. I placed the case on my lap and headed his way, Reggie trotting behind me.

"Hey. Over here." The man turned. I held up the briefcase. "Is this yours?"

He checked the grass at his feet, then looked back at me. He strode over and jerked the case from my hands. Turning away, I heard the clasps open and snap shut. He turned back.

Looking at the ends of my knees, then at my dog, who sat beside me wagging his tail, he asked. "How'd you get this?"

"I saw the whole thing," I started. "This kid grabbed your case and took off running. There wasn't much I could do," I said, glancing at my thighs for emphasis. "But Reggie here is a trained guard dog." *If he believed that, we were home free.* "I gave the command, and he tackled the thief."

"Hmmm." The guy scrutinized Reggie, who was doing his best to look like the hero instead of the thief. "I guess I owe you two."

Digging into the front pocket of his imported suit, he pulled out several folded bills and held them out.

Feeling guilty, I shook off the reward. He dropped the money on my lap anyway. "Buy your dog a steak."

"Thanks."

After he'd gone, I looked at the folded bills … all hundreds. "No more stolen burritos for us!"

We rolled out of the park heading for the grocery store. Reggie was on a short leash to make sure he didn't sneak anything extra this time.

Ω

THE GARDENER'S COMPANION

Sitting on the low weeding stool, Gladys talks to the plants around her as she meticulously pulls stalks of foxtail grass coming up in her flower bed.

"You've got to go. And you, and you, and you," she says to the grasses. "But you, you get to stay," she coos to a small feathery seedling that will grow up to be a yarrow with tiny white flowers.

Her gloved hand reaches under the fragrant leaves of the rose sage bush. "I see you hiding under there. You thought the sage would protect you. Well, not today," she whispers, as she plucks three clumps of cheatgrass from under the branches and deposits them in the bucket at her side. She pauses to smell her gloved hand that carries the pungent aroma of the sage.

She stands and moves her stool to another section of the planter filled with California poppies. "How are my orange beauties doing today? I see you created plenty of babies this spring." Small clumps, two inches tall, push up from the soil in dozens of places, promising more flowers in the months ahead. Gladys' eyes are drawn to a tiny pink flower on a single stalk protruding from a flat green plant with nasty little seed pods.

"What do we have here?" Using her hand weeder with the wooden handle worn smooth from years of use, she pries the stubborn weed from the soil. "You thought your pretty little flower could fool me? I'm onto your tricks, you little troublemaker."

"Who are you talking to?" a small voice asks.

"No one," Gladys answers, looking up to find her neighbor's six-year-old daughter standing on the lawn on the other side of her flowerbed. Her hair has been pulled up high into a ponytail revealing a round face with chubby cheeks, a button nose, and rose petal-colored lips. Based on the mismatched outfit and lack of shoes, Gladys guesses that the child dressed herself.

What was her name again?

"I heard you talking to someone. Someone in your garden. Who's in there?" The child bends at the waist, peering into the planter as if she will discover little people or fairies.

126

Adjusting the cord under her chin that holds her straw hat in place, Gladys says, "It's not a who, it's a what."

The child cocks her head and steps onto the low stone wall that separates the lawn in her yard from the flowerbed in Gladys' yard. "What are you talking to?"

Looking around her neighbor's front yard, Gladys sees a pile of toys on the front porch but no adult.

Where is her mother?

Over the twenty years she's lived in the neighborhood, Gladys prided herself on minding her own business. You don't bug me, and I won't bug you, was her motto. She had no interest in the neighborhood gossip, participating in block parties, buying magazines and candy bars from the neighbor kids, or donating to the various fundraisers. After saying "No" enough times, people knew not to ask.

She was cordial enough. If she was in her garden working, which was the only time you'd find her outside, and a neighbor walked by and said, "Good morning," she'd wave and say, "Good Morning," back. The conversation she currently found herself in with a six-year-old, probably qualified as the most extensive she'd had in years.

"I'm talking to my plants and the weeds." To illustrate, she pulled a weed from the bucket and held it up. "A what, not a who."

"Do they talk back?" the child wanted to know, stepping down off the wall into the flowerbed.

Gladys cringes as she watches small feet step between her newly planted purple salvia. The child works her way around two lavender plants and comes to a stop in front of Gladys.

At least she knows not to step on the plants.

She bends down and tilts her head as if she expects to hear something. "I don't hear anything."

"Of course you don't. They're plants. Plants don't talk."

Standing back up, the child asks, "Then why do you talk to them?"

Gladys doesn't have an answer, so she changes the subject. "What is your name?"

"I'm Taylor. And you're Mrs. Crabapple. My daddy calls you Mrs. Crabby Appleton, cause you're crabby sometimes. Crabapple is a funny name… like a crab and an apple got married or something. Did you make up your name?"

Crabby Appleton? Am I really a crabby person? I keep to myself, is all. I wouldn't say I was crabby.

"No, I didn't make up the name. That's not how last names work. Crabapple was my husband's name, his father's name, and his grandfather's name. When I got married, I took his name, which is what you did back then, but not so much these days."

128

Why am I explaining all this to a little kid?

"Don't you need to be somewhere?" Gladys asks, hoping Taylor gets the hint.

"Nope. I'm supposed to stay outside until lunchtime. Mommy is very tired and sleeping."

What kind of mother leaves her six-year-old outside alone while she sleeps? I hope she didn't assume I'd watch her.

While it was a fairly safe neighborhood and their two houses were at the end of a cul de sac, she certainly wouldn't have left her son outside alone all morning.

"Would you like to help me pick weeds?" When Taylor looks doubtful, she adds, "It's kind of fun, especially if you talk to the plants."

That seems to be the deal clencher. "How do I know which ones are weeds and what do I say to them?"

"Here. See these tall grasses? They are easy to pull out. You can say mean things to them since we don't like them in my flower bed."

Taylor finds a clump of cheatgrass and pulls off the top, saying, "You are a very bad weed."

"No, no, no. It doesn't count if you don't get the root. Look. Grab the clump down by the dirt and then pull it straight up, like this." Gladys demonstrates by saying, "We don't want you here."

Taylor finds another clump and copies Gladys' technique. "You don't belong here, bad weed." She holds up the plant and shows Gladys the root. "Like this?"

"Yes. Make a little pile and I'll pay you five cents for every clump, as long as it has its roots."

At the thought of being paid, Taylor's enthusiasm doubles. "Okay."

Gladys points to the long planter running alongside the opposite side of the yard. "Why don't you work over there."

"Okay." Taylor steps out of the flower bed and skips across the front yard, managing to miss the decorative logs and boulders, before jumping into the other planter.

"Watch out for the plants. Only pull the grasses and nothing else," Gladys shouts, already regretting her decision to give the child a job.

Gladys resumes her weeding, glancing over every few minutes at Taylor. She can't repress her smile as she listens to Taylor berate the weeds.

"You are a naughty girl. You don't belong here." And "You can't hide from me you sneaky little weed." And Gladys' favorite, "Sorry, you gotta go."

About an hour later, an alarm sounds from the vicinity of the flower bed. Gladys turns to see Taylor appear from behind a rose bush and push a button on her watch. "Lunchtime," Taylor sings out. "Should I bring you my weeds?"

"No. I'll come over there." Gladys stands, arching her back to get out the kinks, grabs her bucket and stool, and joins Taylor. "Let's see what I owe you."

There are eight piles of cheatgrass. Gladys is impressed. She didn't think Taylor would get so much done. "Bring me a pile and I'll count."

Sitting on the stool, Gladys adds each clump to her bucket. "One hundred and fifty-two, one hundred and fifty-three. I'm going to owe you a lot of money."

Taylor claps her hands. "How much?"

"I don't know. Let me use a calculator." Gladys pulled her phone out of her back pocket. "Seven dollars and sixty-five cents."

"Wow. That's a lot."

Looking at the flower bed, Gladys is surprised to admit that she's impressed.

Not bad for a six-year-old. And not a flower trampled.

"You did a good job."

Taylor beams. "I have to go home now and eat lunch. My daddy makes my lunch every morning before he goes to work. He's not as good at making lunches as Mommy, but he's getting better. Then I have to take a nap. Do you want me to come back after my nap?"

Gladys finds herself saying, "Yes. I'll have your money for you then."

"Bye." Taylor runs across the yard, dodging plants, rocks, and shrubs.

"Don't step on the flowers," Gladys calls after her.

"I know!"

"And put on some shoes when you come back."

Taylor waves before racing up the steps and disappearing into her house.

***

At three, Taylor is back, wearing a pair of tennis shoes. Gladys notices and nods her approval.

"A real gardener wears shoes. And a hat. Would you like to wear a hat like mine?" Gladys points to a straw hat sitting on a rock in the middle of the yard.

"Oh, sure."

The hat is too large, but Gladys cinches the cord under Taylor's chin, and it stays in place. "Do you want to weed some more, or should I pay you now?"

"More. I like yelling at the weeds. They can't yell back."

"Great. You can work on that planter." Gladys is happy Taylor is wearing shorts. "You might need to get down on your knees to find the grasses under the big lavender plants. We can wash your knees before you go home."

"That's okay. I take a bath every night. Daddy says if you're not dirty then you didn't have any fun." Taylor holds up her hands, still dirty from the morning. "I'm having lots of fun today."

Oh, dear. I should have washed her hands and feet before I sent her home for lunch.

Taylor steps into the planter. "Ready or not, here I come."

Thirty minutes later, Taylor finishes and brings three piles over to Gladys to count. "Smell my hands." Taylor extends her hands until they are almost touching Gladys' face.

"That's lavender. Do you like how it smells?"

Taylor brings her hands to her nose and sniffs. "Oh, yes. I like lavender"

There are not as many grass clumps as in the morning but enough to earn Taylor a total of eight dollars and twenty-five cents. Gladys rounds up and hands Taylor ten one-dollar bills. Taylor's eyes open wide as Gladys counts out the bills one at a time.

"What are you going to do with all your money?"

Taylor's brow furrows as she thinks. Then her face brightens. "I want to do something nice for mommy. Something to make her happy again."

"Why isn't your mom happy?"

Taylor looks down at her feet. "She's sad because of the baby."

Baby? What baby? How did she not notice her neighbor was pregnant?

"What baby? Do you have a new brother or sister?"

Taylor shakes her head. "There was a baby in Mommy's tummy, but now it's gone."

Oh, dear. The woman has had a miscarriage. I didn't even know she was pregnant, although how would I? I barely say two words to her and her husband.

Gladys had had two miscarriages before she carried her one and only son to term. It had been a horrible time… a rollercoaster of hope and despair. Their marriage had barely survived. But with the birth of Jonathan, those terrible years were soon forgotten, or so it seemed. Learning of her neighbor's miscarriage brought the pain back as if it were only yesterday.

"What do you think would make your mom happy?"

"Flowers. She likes flowers. Can you help me buy flowers?" Taylor holds out her money.

Gladys looks over at her neighbor's yard. Except for the green grass, that needs cutting, there isn't a spot of color to be found. A concrete path leading to the front door divides the lawn into two equal squares. Concrete steps rise to a wooden porch. No porch swing. No potted plants. It's almost like no one lives there.

"How would you like it if we plant some flowers like the ones in my yard? You could water them and keep the weeds out. Then the flowers would last longer. Do you think your mom would like that?"

"Oh, yes." Taylor hands the ten dollars back. "Can you buy them for me? And lavender, too."

"Sure. But first, I'm going to ask your dad if it's okay. We are going to need to remove some of your lawn."

"You could ask my mom. She's home now," Taylor suggests, hoping to get started right away.

"Let's make it a surprise. I'll talk to your dad when he comes home from work. If he says yes, I'll go to the store tomorrow morning and we can get started after your nap. How does that sound?"

Taylor jumps up and down clapping her hands, making a high-pitched squeal that Gladys thinks might be able to break glass.

"I take that as a yes."

***

The next day, Taylor opens her front door to find Gladys removing grass along the edge of the concrete walkway. The right side is already finished, with squares of grass setting off to the side. "Mrs. Crabapple! Dad said yes?"

"No. I'm destroying your lawn for the fun of it." Taylor is shocked. "I'm kidding. He said yes."

There's that high-pitched squeal again. No wonder her mom wants her outside.

Taylor comes down the steps and joins Gladys. "Watch out for the string."

Taylor looks around until she finds two strings running from the porch steps to the sidewalk, parallel to the walkway. "What are they for?"

"The string marks the new planter and makes sure I cut the grass in a straight line."

Taylor looks at the large shovel in Gladys' hand. "Can I use that to cut the grass?"

"You're not tall or heavy enough to use this shovel." Seeing the disappointment on Taylor's face, Gladys adds, "Don't worry. I have a special job for you." Gladys puts down the shovel. "Follow me."

Taylor follows as Gladys heads to the tree in her front yard. Under the tree are sixteen, one-gallon containers—eight lavenders and eight African daisies in various shades of pink. Four bags of soil amendment, a small purple watering can, two shiny purple ceramic pots, and a small straw gardening hat with matching gloves round out the supplies.

"My ten dollars bought all of this?" Taylor runs up to the hat and gloves. "Are these for me?"

"Yes."

No need to tell the kid that her father slipped me a hundred and I made up the rest. Neither father nor daughter have a clue how much plants cost these days.

It doesn't matter to Gladys. For once her neighbor's yard will be nice to look at and she's doing something nice to cheer up Taylor's mom. What Gladys isn't ready to admit to herself is by helping her neighbor she's helping herself. For the first time since Harold died, she actually feels useful.

Taylor puts on her new hat and gloves. "How do I look?"

"Like a real gardener. For your first task, you need to bring the pots over and line them up on the walkway. Same number of plants on each side. Four lavenders on each side with a daisy in between. Got it?"

"I think so." Taylor wraps her skinny arms around the first pot and lifts it, hugging it to her chest.

"Is it too heavy?" Gladys asks as she watches Taylor walk down the path to the sidewalk.

"Nope," she shouts out and continues around the lawn.

That should keep her occupied for now.

While Gladys works on removing the rest of the lawn, Taylor moves back and forth, bringing all the plants over to her yard and arranging them along the walkway.

"Space them out evenly. You have them all bunched up." Gladys sits on the porch steps and watches Taylor work out the spacing. "That looks better," she encourages.

"Now what?"

The bags of soil amendment are too heavy for the child and even too heavy for her. She'll ask Dan to move them over when he gets home. "We need to throw the old grass away but first we have to shake off all the dirt. Do you want to do that?"

Taylor picks up a square of grass with two hands and shakes it with gusto, causing dirt to rain down. "Like this?"

"Yes, but do it over the dirt, not the grass."

Exhausted from digging out the lawn, Gladys is happy to watch Taylor shake the dirt off the roots. Taylor finishes before Gladys is ready to stand again.

"Now what?"

Boy. I wish I had half her energy.

"We should throw all the grass away. I'll go get a trash can," Gladys says, starting to push herself off the steps.

"We have one. It's empty. I can get it." Without waiting for Gladys to reply, Taylor runs to the side of the house next to the garage and moments later comes around the corner dragging a large plastic trash barrel.

Gladys watches as Taylor slam dunks squares of grass into the barrel, adding farewells to each clump. "So long." "Bye-bye." "Don't come back."

For the first time in as long as she can remember, Gladys begins to laugh. Not a girlish giggle, not a repressed Ha Ha, but a full-blown guffaw that shakes her entire body and brings tears to her eyes.

I've created a monster.

***

It takes the two gardeners—one older and slow, the other younger and quick—two more days to amend the soil, dig the holes, then plant the lavender and daisies, including filling the two purple pots with daisies and setting them on the porch on either side of the front door.

Gladys shows Taylor how to fill the watering can and carefully fill each of the depressions around each plant with water. Two large bags of mulch are delivered and dropped on the driveway where Gladys and Taylor bring a bucketful at a time to the new flowerbeds and spread it out over the bare dirt and around each plant to keep in the moisture.

Standing and brushing off their hands in unison, a passing stranger might mistake them for grandmother and granddaughter, wearing matching straw hats, cloth gloves, and mannerisms.

Surveying their work, Gladys is filled with a feeling of pride and something else she can't quite put her finger on. She puts her arm down and pulls Taylor close to her.

"We did good, kiddo."

Taylor wraps her arms around Gladys' leg. "Can I go get mom now?"

"Sure."

Taylor releases Gladys' leg and races up the walkway, up the steps, and disappears into the house. Gladys suddenly feels odd. Should she stay? Should she go? She looks around. There's nothing left to do, so she walks back to her yard, suddenly tired, ready to disappear once again back into her house.

Gloves and hat off, hands washed, she gulps down a glass of cold water standing at the sink. She settles on the stool at the counter and opens the paper, ready to catch up on the latest news, when a knock at the door has her getting up again.

She peeps through the peephole to see Taylor and her mom.

What is her name? Damn my memory.

As she's opening the door, Taylor starts talking. "Here she is, Mrs. Crabapple, not Mrs. Crabby Appleton. She's really nice. She helped me plant our garden and showed me how to water the plants, so you don't have to do anything." Then looking up at her mom, she takes her hand and says, "And this is my mom."

"We've met before." *Not often enough that I can remember her damn name.* "Would you like to come in?" Gladys steps aside to let them enter.

Taylor takes a step, but her mother holds her back. "Thank you, but we can't stay. I just wanted to tell you how much I appreciate what you did for Taylor, letting her work in your yard and ours." The woman looks down at her daughter who is still wearing her hat and gloves. "The new planters are beautiful. I love the lavender. It's quite the transformation both of the yard and…"

Gladys nods. "I understand. If there is anything I can do, please—"

"I'm fine," the woman says abruptly. "Thank you again, Mrs. Crabapple."

"Please call me Gladys."

"Okay, Gladys. And you can call me Jill."

Oh, thank god, she said her name.

"Let's go, Taylor. We don't want to bother Gladys any longer." Jill says as she turns to leave.

Gladys makes a decision. "Taylor. Would you mind grabbing your watering can and watering my daisies? They are looking a bit droopy."

"Sure." Taylor pulls free from her mother's hand and sprints across the yard.

"I wanted to say something before you leave," Gladys starts. "I know how devastated you are."

Jill doesn't react. Just another platitude by a well-meaning neighbor.

"I know because I lost two children. One at three and one at five months pregnant."

Jill turns around and faces Gladys. "How did you go on? Most days, I don't even want to get out of bed. I know it's not fair to Taylor, but I just can't."

"I know. I was inconsolable for months. And it didn't help that people said the stupidest things. If one more person told me, 'Oh, you can try again,' I might currently be serving time for murder."

That made Jill smile.

"You lost a child. You're in mourning. There is no timeline or right way to work through this. I'm sorry I don't have a magic pill or something. But I wanted you to know that I'm here if you want to talk. I found that no one wanted to talk about the two boys I lost. They didn't know what to say or how to act, so they pretended they never existed, which was worse. It made me feel like I was the oddball for wanting to acknowledge their existence. They were my babies…" Gladys can't finish her sentence as she sniffs back tears.

The next thing she knows, Jill has wrapped her in an embrace, and they are both crying. Jill whispers, "Thank you, thank you, thank you."

When their tears are finally spent, the two mothers lock their eyes. They understand each other, and without saying a word, it's understood that they will look out for each other from here on.

***

Four months later, Gladys walks up the pathway to Jill's front door. The lavender is blooming, making the journey an aromatic delight. The once-barren front porch is alive with color. Jill has added several colorful pots of varying sizes and filled them with a collection of soft pink roses, deep purple salvia, and white geraniums. Gladys approves of the color choices—no shocking reds, oranges, or yellows, to distract the eye.

Very calming.

At the top of the steps, Gladys knocks gently on the door. She hears a high-pitched squeal of delight followed by, "She's here."

The door is flung open, and Taylor greets her, wearing her gardening hat and gloves. "Come in, come in, come in." She takes Gladys by the hand and pulls her in and down the hallway. "Daddy's made a new planter in the backyard and we're going to plant vegetables… carrots, potatoes, beans, and tomatoes. Come on."

Jill and her husband Dan are in the kitchen, but Taylor and Gladys don't stop as they pass through to the backdoor.

"Hi and bye," Dan says with a laugh.

"I'll bring you a glass of wine," Jill offers.

Out in the yard, Taylor is talking rapid-fire, explaining where she is going to plant everything, how they are going to tape the seed packs to sticks and poke them in the ground, and how she has a new watering can just for the backyard, and how Gladys will have to come over for dinner again when they have carrots and potatoes.

Jill and Dan join them, handing Gladys a glass of red wine. "We have quite the little gardener now, thanks to you."

"I've created a monster," Gladys says, as they listen to Taylor go on and on.

Jill nods. "Yes. Such a lovely little monster."

THE MACHINES AWAKEN

A heavy layer of silence presses down on the house like a thick, warm blanket. Nothing stirs. Nothing moves as the planet turns, bringing the sun closer to the horizon. A solitary robin atop a birch tree in the predawn light announces the imminent arrival of the fiery orb. A chatty mockingbird joins in as the sun crests the grass-covered hills to the east of the bucolic neighborhood.

At precisely 7 am, the simultaneous whirling of fifteen tiny motors is the first sound of the house awakening as the shades begin their morning ascent, rising to the top of the window casing, letting soft yellow light flood each room.

In the kitchen, a soft "click" indicates the coffee maker has begun its task of heating water and brewing coffee. Off in the primary bedroom, the radio alarm clock switches on filling the room with the voice of the local newscaster with the traffic and weather report, followed by the top 40 hits.

A "whoosh" of gas igniting signals the hot water heater has come to life, guaranteeing the water will be up to temperature for a morning shower. Outside, cars pass on the street, their passengers heading to work or ferrying children to school. A dog barks as a group of kids with bookbags, and sack lunches walk past on their way to the bus stop. Sparrows and house finches twitter and chirp as they go about their business of catching insects and attracting mates.

At 8:00 am, two automated vacuums—one upstairs and one downstairs—disengage from their charging ports and begin their prescribed routes around furniture through their designated rooms. An hour later, they will return to their stations, click into place, and charge up for another day.

The automated sprinkler system kicks into gear at 8:30, popping up sprinkler heads to mist the lawn with a gentle rain. Twenty minutes later, the lawn glistens in the morning sun and the sprinklers disappear as the water is diverted to the bubblers hidden in the rose beds. The robin descends from its perch to pull worms from the moist lawn.

A text message triggers a high-pitched ping on the cellphone plugged in next to the bed. At 10:02, the phone rings with the sound of windchimes dancing in the wind. The call goes to voicemail.

As the house heats up, the air conditioner switches on with the intention of keeping the rooms at a pleasant 72 degrees. The cooled air pouring through the vents and the occasional text message alert are the only sounds echoing off the walls. Around 1:00 pm, an alert sounds from the phone, "Person detected," followed by the "squeak" of metal and the "plop" of mail hitting the tile floor. A disembodied voice announces, "You are being recorded."

Around 3:00 pm, the phone announces again, "Person detected," as someone knocks on the door. The security camera captures an image of a group of three people—two women dressed in long dresses and a man dressed in a suit—all holding pamphlets. The system warns the visitors that they are being recorded. They don't seem to mind and knock again. When no one answers, they walk past the rose beds to the sidewalk, heading off to the neighbor's house.

As the sun drops below the horizon, two porch lights switch on, casting a circle of warm light around the front door and the wooden swing that hangs from two chains. The swing creeks and sways gently in the soft evening breeze. Inside, a table lamp in the living room clicks on as the shades begin their descent for the evening. At 7, the television pops on and will stay on until 10, airing local news and a two-hour movie.

Around 8, the cellphone rings three times before going to voicemail. A ping indicates a new text message has been received. At 10:15, the table lamp switches off while upstairs, a bedside lamp clicks on. Finally, at 11 pm, the lamp clicks off and the room is plunged into darkness. Downstairs, the peaceful hum of the refrigerator lulls the house to sleep.

A new day dawns. Shades roll up, coffee is brewed, the lawn is watered. Another phone call goes to voicemail. More pings as text messages arrive. Downstairs, a new sound… a female voice reverberates through the kitchen, bouncing off the walls.

"Hey, Dad. I thought you were coming home from your trip on Monday. Maybe I have that wrong. I'll double check my calendar. Did you lose your phone again? I've called and texted and you're not answering. I'm glad you have this landline. Call me when you're home."

Mail drops through the slot in the door as the air conditioner cycles on and off in its quest to keep the temperature steady. The voice returns.

"Hey, Dad. I checked the calendar. You should have come home two days ago. I also checked your flights. No delays. Did you change your plans? Where are you? I'm starting to get worried. Call me back."

Night and the shades descend. Lights click on, the new broadcaster reports trouble in the Middle East followed by a cheerful weather woman promising another cloudless day and high temperatures.

An owl hoots. Another answers. The neighborhood dogs start a conversation with yips and barks until they are called inside by their owners. Crickets fill in the void as a full moon peeks over the hills and bathes the neighborhood in its pale white light. A cat pads silently along the top of a block wall, on the prowl.

Seven am. The shades rise, the radio announces an accident on the freeway as coffee brews, the brown liquid threatening to overflow the pot. At eight, "Person detected" sounds. A key slides into the lock, the knob is turned. As the door swings open, it pushes the pile of mail to one side.

"Dad."

Except for the whirls of the automated vacuums, the house is silent.

"Dad," the woman calls out, louder this time, before gathering the mail.

As she heads to the kitchen, she checks the living room.

"Shit!" she exclaims, startled by the large, round black circle coming out from behind the couch and heading down the hall.

"Stupid vacuum," she exhales, calming her nerves. "Dad." Still no answer.

In the kitchen, she sets the mail on the counter, unplugs the coffee pot and dumps the coffee down the sink. There are no used coffee cups setting out, no wet spoon, no dirty dishes in the sink.

She calls again as she climbs the stairs, her voice shriller and more urgent. "Dad."

At the doorway to her father's room, she pauses. A suitcase stands like a sentinel next to the undisturbed bed, the decorative red pillows placed in a small huddle, just like her mother used to do it.

Stepping inside, she sees her father's phone on the bedside table, plugged into the wall. Dread creeps up her spine as she takes a second step. There is a whirling sound coming from the other side of the bed. Three more steps and she sees him.

Fully clothed her father lies on the carpet, face down. She freezes, her breath leaving her. The automated vacuum has cleaned around her father, leaving a perfect line around his body like the chalk outline you'd find at the scene of a crime.

She kneels. She exhales a breath along with a single, barely audible word, "Dad."

"Siri. Call 911."

Her Dad's phone lights up. "This is 911. What is your emergency."

She places her hand on her father's back.
Nothing stirs. Nothing moves as the planet turns,
bringing the sun higher. A shaft of light slants into the
room, placing a spotlight on her father. The woman
sobs. The vacuum whirls as it makes its way around her
and leaves her with her grief.

$$\Omega$$

FALL

Autumn leaves skip and dance along the park sidewalk like children running out to recess. The pigeons peck at the breadcrumbs I've sprinkled, their heads moving back and forward with every step … entertaining. The pigeons pause.

The boy and his dog approach … the dog pulling, leash taunt, the boy—eyes glued to his phone's screen—oblivious to the disruption he causes each day when he walks his dog. The dog scatters the pigeons. Tired of the disturbance, I lower my cane between dog and owner like a toll barrier.

Patting the bench, "Sit," I command.

The dog sits, the boy doesn't. The dog has been well trained. I can't say the same for the boy.

"SIT." He complies warily.

I pass him the bag of breadcrumbs, motioning him to toss them. Breadcrumbs take flight. The pigeons return and with them a smile as we watch the birds peck.

Ω

SHORTY AND ME

At four feet, eleven inches, I'm an inch too tall to be considered a dwarf ... the first and only time I've been too tall to qualify for something.

As a kid, everyone was short. Then in sixth grade, friends started shooting up like stocks of corn, while I stayed down with the cabbages. That's when the teasing started. Being different means, you have a target on your back, sometimes literally, like the time a "friend" taped a sign to my shirt saying, "Go back to Hobbiton." After that, kids called me, "Hobbit." Since Frodo and Samwise Ganges were my heroes—short fellas save the day—I didn't mind. Then kids switched to names like Shrimp, Tiny, Oompa Lumpa, and the ever-popular Shorty.

Complaining about the name-calling to my five-foot-two Italian father elicited this advice. "If you're gonna fight, make sure you take the first punch and punch 'em in the balls. Otherwise, say something funny then while they're laughing, walk away."

After receiving detention and a black eye for punching a bully in the nuts—to which my father said, "Good for you."—I changed strategies, using humor to deflect the insults.

My high school plan was to lay low. But lying low wasn't an option for my polar opposite, Connor Clark. While I prayed for a massive growth spurt, Connor viewed the world from a different altitude. At six-foot-six, not only was he the tallest guy in our class, but the tallest guy in the school, including teachers and coaches.

The first time I saw him amble down the hall I thought, "Wow!" I must have spoken aloud because he responded with an easy, "Hey."

"You're so tall." Statement of the obvious.

"You're so short," he shot back with a lopsided grin, never breaking his stride.

I caught up with him at the Freshman lockers where he was doubled over working the combination on a bottom locker. My locker—two over, on the top row—had me stretching on tiptoes, arms over my head.

"Life is cruel, right?"

Connor turned, assessed the situation with his puppy dog eyes, and agreed.

"We should switch lockers," I suggested.

Connor straightened, now towering over me. I felt like an ant being examined by a giraffe.

Intimidating.

A crease appeared across his brow. "I don't think that's allowed."

"I won't tell if you don't," I tried.

I watched as he considered the pros and cons. Con … if I hid contraband in my locker, the one assigned to Connor, he would be blamed. Pro … he wouldn't have to bend over for an entire year. Ready to shrug off my suggestion and continue my struggle, he surprised me by holding out his hand.

"Deal." My hand disappeared in his for a quick shake, a pact of trust between two misfits. "I'm Connor."

"Leo," I said sporting a stupid grin.

We fumbled around switching lockers before the warning bell rang. "See you at lunch?" Connor asked.

"Sure." Had I really made a friend on day one? "I bring a sack lunch," I blurted out, raising my defenses to fend off the condescending attitude sure to come my way like I'd experienced in middle school.

"Me, too. Cafeteria food is gross."

A sigh of relief. "Exactly." I'd found a kindred soul trapped in a body as different from mine as corn and cabbage.

***

Throughout high school, we only shared a couple of classes since he was super smart and me, not so much. I had a brilliant idea. The two of us should try out for the volleyball team. Connor, perfect for obvious reasons, could spike the ball straight down and put up an impenetrable wall at the net. And me? There's a position for someone of my stature … libero, a defensive back row specialist tasked with digging the ball. Practically on the floor already, I was made for this position.

At tryouts, the coaches wanted to bump Connor up to JV, even though he'd never played volleyball. Here we go, I thought. The end of our friendship. Connor will be a superstar and I'll be left behind.

Connor looked at me and then at the other freshman. "This is my team," he said simply, and that was that.

Our promise to stick together had survived its first challenge. I learned that not only was Connor a loyal, gentle giant, but we shared a common concern, which we bemoaned while sitting in the bleachers at the freshman dance … would we ever find a girl who didn't freak out about our height?

After winning our first match handily, two guys from the other team snarked, "Way to go, Stretch," and to me, "Nice job, Shorty." Not very original, but what do you expect from pubescent high school boys? As a joke,

I started calling Connor "Shorty" and he reciprocated calling me "Stretch," preempting the insults and based on the puzzled looks, creating confusion among the haters. While the basketball coaches pulled out their hair wondering why Connor "wasted" his time with volleyball, we kept winning, and with Connor as my wingman, I never got roughed up again.

After graduation, we went our separate ways, Connor to UCLA on a volleyball AND scholastic scholarship and me to Columbia College in Chicago where I enrolled in the Comedy Writing and Performance program. Turned out that my self-deprecating humor could be turned into a career. Through the years, we kept in touch, starting every communication with, "Hey, Shorty. Hey Stretch."

Today, I'm married to a woman a foot taller than me, and together we've managed to create a couple of kids of average height. The day my daughter was born, Connor showed up at the hospital with a sign that read, "Way to go, Stretch!"

This summer, Connor will be playing two-man beach volleyball at the Summer Olympics for Team USA. I plan to be there with a sign that reads, "Way to go, Shorty."

No one will have a clue, except Shorty and me.

GIRL UNDER THE TABLE

It started with a phone call after dinner. Megan's mom cried out, put her face into her hands, and sobbed.

Megan's dad rushed to her side. "What is it? What's wrong?"

"It's Ronnie. He's … he's … gone."

This scared Megan, so she did what she always did when she was scared: she hid under the big wooden table in the dining room. It took a long time before her parents noticed she was gone. When her father called for her, Megan didn't answer at first. She knew if she stayed under the table, she'd be safe.

Megan watched as her father's legs came closer. He pulled a chair out, lifted the edge of the tablecloth, and peeked under the table.

"There you are," he said, but not in the same excited way he'd say the same words when they were playing hide and go seek. "Time for bed, Kiddo." He held out his hand.

Something scary had happened. She could hear her mom on the phone, talking and crying at the same time. Her dad's eyes were red and puffy, and his mouth made a straight line across his face. Megan shook her head.

"Come on, now. Bedtime."

Megan hugged her knees. "What's wrong with Mommy?"

Her dad dropped to his hands and knees. He exhaled a long breath. "She's sad. Now come on." He held out his hand again. This time Megan took it and let her father pull her out.

"Why is she sad?" Megan asked as she followed her father up the stairs.

"Not now, Kiddo. Let's just get you all tucked in. Everything will be fine in the morning."

But it wasn't fine in the morning, or the next day, or the next. Five days later, Megan sat under the table again. Her favorite blue dress with the white ruffles made a circle on the carpet around her. Her floppy-eared rabbit lay in her lap as she stroked the smooth satin edging of her blue blankie. Some kind of party moved and swirled around the table above her. It wasn't a happy party like a birthday party, but a sad party, with adults sniffing back tears, and people saying, "I'm sorry for your loss." She knew two things. Her Uncle Ronnie was gone; something was lost.

Maybe it's Uncle Ronnie who is lost.

That made her sad because Uncle Ronnie, with his booming voice and strong arms, liked to swing her around in a circle. It made her feel like she was flying.

People arrived with food, placing casserole dishes, trays of cookies, salads, and bread on the table above her. The rich smell of chocolate brownies tempted Megan to venture from her hiding spot until she heard an adult whisper something about a "terrible tragedy."

What Megan heard didn't make sense and frightened her even more. Aunty Josey tried to coax her to join the party with the promise of her favorite sandwich … peanut butter and bananas, to no avail. Megan stayed silent and hugged her rabbit tight.

If I'm quiet, no one will know I'm here. I'll be safe from the terrible tragedy.

Her mother, wearing the black pumps Megan liked to try on, stood next to the table. "Could you make sure Megan eats something? I need to lie down," she said to someone Megan couldn't see.

A minute later, a corner of the tablecloth lifted, and Megan's father's face peered at her.

"There you are," he said. "What are you doing under there?"

"Hiding," Megan said barely above a whisper.

"Can I hide with you?" her father asked.

Megan nodded.

Her father lifted the tablecloth and crawled under the table. He couldn't sit up straight because he was too big. He had to tilt his head to the side. "What are we hiding from?" he asked.

"Scary things," Megan whispered, looking out at the legs gathered around the edge of the table.

"What kind of scary things?" her father wanted to know. "Lions? Monsters? Ghosts?"

Megan shook her head. "Things that make big people cry."

"Oh, *those* things," her father nodded. "I know all about *those* things."

Megan looked at her father. His eyes didn't twinkle like they usually did, especially when they were playing the tickle game or hide and seek, but he wasn't crying like her mother. She crawled into her father's lap, and he wrapped his arms around her. They sat under the table for a good long time. More people arrived with food, and still they sat under the table. Someone must have brought an apple pie because they could smell the sweet apples and cinnamon.

Megan's father asked, "Are you hungry?"

Megan shook her head and pressed herself into her father's chest.

"Are you thirsty? I could bring you a glass of milk," her father offered, and started to move.

"No. Don't go." Megan rubbed her face into her father's shirt.

"Okay. I'll stay as long as you want," her father reassured her.

"Good," Megan said, and pressed her ear to her father's chest until she could hear his heartbeat. After a few minutes, she asked, "Why is Mommy crying?"

"Her brother Ronnie was in a bad accident. It makes her sad."

"I was in an accident, too." Megan showed her father a bright red mark on her knee.

"I remember. You fell walking down the stairs. I bet that hurt," he said, rubbing the red spot.

Megan nodded.

"Your Uncle Ronnie was in a bigger accident."

"Is that why he turned into a vegetable?" Megan wondered out loud.

"Where did you hear that?" her father wanted to know.

Megan pointed up. "Mrs. Clark was whispering to Mr. Clark about Uncle Ronnie being a vegetable. What kind of vegetable? Did he turn into broccoli? I don't like broccoli. If I eat broccoli, will I turn into a vegetable, too?"

"No," her father chuckled. "Eating vegetables makes you healthy and strong. Your Uncle Ronnie hit his head really hard in the accident and couldn't think right anymore. He didn't turn into a vegetable."

"Did he turn into a toaster or a television?" Megan asked.

Her father laughed softly again, and it vibrated his chest. Megan liked it when her father laughed.

"No. Why do you think that?"

"Because I heard a man, wearing shiny black shoes, say, 'They pulled the plug on Uncle Ronnie.' People don't have plugs, so he must have turned into something with a cord like a toaster."

Megan's father took a deep, shuddering breath. Megan's head and body rose and fell with the swell of his chest. "Uncle Ronnie did not turn into a toaster. At the hospital, they used a machine to help him breathe. They unplugged the machine, not Uncle Ronnie."

"Oh, that's better," Megan sighed. "I'm glad he's not a toaster."

"Me, too," her father said gravely.

While knowing that her Uncle wasn't a vegetable or a toaster made Megan feel better, she still had more questions. "Daddy?"

"Yes, Megan."

"I heard Grandma say that Uncle Ronnie was in a better place. Can we go visit him? Will that make Mommy stop crying?"

"No, I'm sorry, Sweetie. Uncle Ronnie didn't go to a place we can visit. He died," her father said softly.

Megan thought about that. "Like my goldfish Albert died?" she asked.

"Yes, like your goldfish," her father agreed.

"Are you going to flush Uncle Ronnie down the toilet, too?" Megan couldn't imagine how her Uncle, who was taller than her father, would ever fit in the toilet.

"No, Megan. That's just for goldfish."

They sat in silence as the buzzing of hushed conversations swirled around them. The high-pitch clinking of silverware against her mother's China dishes punctuated the din as people walked around the table serving themselves.

"What will they do with Uncle Ronnie?" Megan wanted to know.

"We will bury him," her father said quietly.

"In the dirt?" Megan didn't like how that sounded. She imagined her father digging a big hole in the backyard like he did when he planted the new apple tree.

"First, we will lay him in a beautiful box and then we will bury the box," her father explained.

"Like we buried my hamster Freddy in the shoe box?" Megan had placed an old cloth napkin in the box for Freddy. She added flowers she'd picked from the backyard, and his favorite hamster kibble.

"Yes, like Freddy, but the box will be bigger and made of wood," her father explained.

Megan thought about that for a minute. "Uncle Ronnie will like that better."

"I think so, too," her father agreed.

Father and daughter sat under the table in silence. The front door opened, and a gust of wind ruffled the edges of the tablecloth, sending three scarlet and yellow leaves tumbling between people's feet until they came to rest under the table. Megan tilted her head back to look at her father.

"Daddy?"

"Yes, Megan."

"Are you and Mommy going to die?" she asked in a tiny voice.

"Someday, but not today," her father said, picking up one of the leaves and swirling it between his fingers.

"Will Grandma and Grandpa die?" Megan asked.

"Someday, but not today," her father said again, handing his daughter the leaf.

Megan placed the leaf on her father's leg and smoothed it out until it was flat. "Will I die?" Megan asked.

"Someday, but not today," her father said and gave her a big squeeze. "Everything living dies someday. It happens to animals and plants and people," he said softly. "It's like this leaf. Remember when the tree was full of green leaves?"

Megan didn't move. Her father continued. "You know how the leaves are turning yellow, and red, and brown. Their time to be green is over. It's time for them to fly away in the wind. But it's not your time, or my time, or Mommy's time yet."

"It was Uncle Ronnie's time?"

"Yes, like a beautiful leaf."

As Megan thought about a yellow leaf flying away, a warm drop of water splashed on her forehead, and her father sniffed. Then her stomach made a funny sound like a lion roaring.

"I'm hungry," she said.

"Me, too. Would you like to have a peanut butter and banana sandwich?" her father asked.

Megan smiled for the first time all day. She climbed out of her father's lap, and together they crawled out from under the table.

NOT A ZOMBIE APOCALYPSE

It started with the chipmunks. As fall leaves drifted to the ground, the chipmunks were busy robbing the bird feeders and stuffing their cheeks with seeds.

"Greedy little bastards," Frannie grumbled as she filled the bird feeder once again. "How can such a little creature eat so much?"

Curious, Frannie googled chipmunk behavior and learned that they were not eating all that seed, but were storing it in their burrows for winter, which got her thinking … maybe she should store food for the winter, too. It wasn't unheard of for a winter storm to roar into the mountains, dump a couple of feet of snow, shut down the power with high winds, and then vanish, leaving the residents snowed in without power. Since living in the mountains, they had been snowed in only a half dozen times, and usually only for a couple of days. They had had plenty of food and were in no danger of starving. But what if something else happened and they needed to be self-sufficient for a couple of weeks or months? What then?

In researching "preparing for disasters," Frannie discovered the world of preppers.

Who knew?

When she mentioned the idea of prepping to her husband, Harold, had laughed, saying, "Those guys are a bunch of kooks and nuts. They spend all their time and money on getting ready for a Zombie Apocalypse that is never going to happen."

Well, maybe not Zombies.

She never mentioned it again, but she did start preparing. Hope for the best, prepare for the worst, she thought as she added four cans of baked beans to her shopping cart and an extra gallon of water. Her plan … buy a few extra items each month.

But where can I store everything? Where were places Harold would never look?

That's when she hired Benny. Benny, a strange young man who lived alone across the street, didn't seem to have any friends, and he never talked to Harold, which was key. She knew he liked to build stuff because she could see him in his garage at all times of the day making bird and dog houses, and elaborate structures for cats. He sold his creations at the local farmer's market. As far as she knew, this was his only job.

Harold played golf on Tuesdays and Thursdays, leaving the house Harold-free for at least four hours. That's when she'd have Benny build her hidden storage spaces … a sliding box hidden under the couches in both the living room and the family room; a large box the exact size and shape as the box springs under the mattresses in each of the bedrooms except the primary bedroom; and false walls with storage behind them in her gardening shed in the back yard.

Getting Benny to talk to her had been the most difficult part of her plan. Every time she started to walk across the street, he'd disappear into his house and wouldn't answer the door when she knocked. Finally, she wrote him a letter and left it on his workbench in the garage. Two days later, she tried again, and this time he didn't disappear and waited for her.

When she entered the garage, he handed her a notepad. Frannie read the following: Yes, I will build the storage cabinets. I charge $60 an hour plus materials. I can work when Harold is not home. I will take the measurements, build the cabinets here, and then bring them over. I don't talk because I can't, not because I don't want to.

Frannie looked up. She wondered why he couldn't talk. Wondered what had happened, but didn't want to pry. She figured if he had wanted her to know, he would have written that down, too.

"Sounds like a plan. I'll pay you right away for materials. You buy what you need and give me the receipt, and I'll give you cash. Harold is gone every Tuesday and Thursday from nine until one playing golf unless the weather is bad. You'll see that his car is gone. Here is my phone number. You can text me if you have questions about something. Does this sound good?"

Benny nodded.

"Great. Oh, and please don't tell anyone about this little project, okay? Especially, Harold."

Benny cocked his head to the side and squinted his eyes at her.

"Don't worry. I'm not doing anything wrong. Just hiding a few essentials. You know … for the Zombie Apocalypse."

Benny snorted, which Frannie interpreted as a laugh.

"We good?"

Benny nodded, then took the pad, scribbled something, and handed it back.

Frannie read and replied, "You could come over now to see what you're up against and take measurements."

Benny followed her across the street. Three weeks later, Glayds had her secret storage compartments.

Grocery store coupons came out every Thursday, so that's when Frannie shopped. The fact that Benny played golf on Thursdays meant she could hide her extra non-perishable items under the bed, the couch, and in her garden shed. Benny had placed the boxes under the couches on rollers, making it easy for Frannie to slide them out and back. He'd fashioned hinges with springs on the beds, similar to the bed with storage underneath in their motor home. A mattress skirt hid the box from view, and since Harold had never changed the sheets on any of the beds in the house, Frannie was confident he'd never notice the box springs had been replaced with a wooden box platform.

It took two years to fill all the spaces she'd created, but as she added the last can of raviolis and bottle of water to the hidden cabinet behind the wall of her garden tools, Frannie breathed a satisfied sigh.

There. It's done.

She read that she should rotate her canned goods and replace the water, so every week, before she went shopping, she'd pull out a couple of cans and place them in the kitchen pantry, buying replacement items as she went. In addition to food and water, Frannie had stocked up on candles, matches, and cans of propane that fit their small camping stove stored in their RV. She'd also gotten cash back whenever she could and had amassed several thousand dollars in cash.

Harold only noticed the slight increase in the grocery bill once when he came home from golf early due to a lightning storm. Luckily, Frannie had already stashed her extra items and was in the middle of putting the cold items in the refrigerator when her husband walked in.

Frannie shrieked in fright. "Oh my god, Harold," she cried, putting her hand to her heart. "You scared me half to death. What are you doing home so early?"

"Lightning. You're kind of jumpy," he said, looking around as if he might find something, but only found grocery bags on the counters.

"Must be the electricity in the air," Frannie offered, grabbing a carton of milk from a bag and sticking her head in the refrigerator to cool her nerves.

That was close.

"Here. Let me help." Harold handed her a dozen eggs and then the orange juice. At the bottom of the bag, he pulled out the receipt. "Wow. $250. That's what we spend on groceries these days?"

Before he could look closer, Frannie pulled the receipt from his hand and started reading off prices. "Eggs are now twelve dollars a dozen, and hamburger is over twelve dollars a pound. Prices are outrageous these days. I paid five dollars for a single avocado! Tell me what to cut out, and I will. No more hamburgers or steaks?"

"Well, we don't need a five-dollar avocado, that's for sure," Harold said, not suggesting they cut any of the items he enjoyed.

"Fine. I won't buy avocados. That will save us tons of money. I'll start having bacon and eggs for breakfast, too."

Harold reconsidered. "That's not what I meant. I guess I'm out of touch with what things cost these days. You can have your avocado."

Thank you, Your Majesty. "Any time you want to 'get in touch' with prices at the market, just let me know and you can do the weekly shopping."

Harold shook his head and grabbed a soda from the still open refrigerator and left the kitchen in defeat.

***

It wasn't a Zombie Apocalypse, but it was bad, real bad. The power went out and didn't come back on. Stores couldn't take credit cards, only cash. ATM's weren't working without electricity, and when they were connected to generators, they quickly ran out of cash and weren't replenished. It didn't take long for gasoline to be the issue. Stores and restaurants locked their doors, and the looting began. The two grocery stores on the mountain were quickly depleted.

Harold wanted to leave the mountain. Frannie refused. They needed to lie low and ride it out. Down the mountain would be even worse. More desperate people doing desperate things.

"Surely, the National Guard and the Military will be called in to set up aid stations in the major cities," he tried. "No one cares about us up here. We're isolated. We'll run out of food."

"No. No, we won't," Frannie insisted in a calm voice that belied the situation.

"We have no idea how long this will last. Without electricity, the food in the fridge will go bad. What are we going to eat, Frannie?"

"We are going to eat all the food in the freezer and refrigerator first—"

"And how do you propose we cook everything without electricity. I knew an all-electric house was a mistake," Harold groused.

Really? I thought you loved the idea.

"How about you use the backyard barbecue to start. Then we can use the stove and oven in the RV that runs on propane. I have four extra propane tanks in the shed. After that, you can build a fire, like the cave man you are," Frannie said, hoping the jab would snap him out of it.

"And then what?" Harold shouted at her.

"Follow me," she said, and headed for the living room. With Harold standing behind her, Frannie knelt, reached underneath the couch until she found the brass handle, and pulled. Out slid the drawer filled with canned goods, boxes of pasta, jars of sauce, bags of beef jerky, jelly, and jams.

She turned and looked up at Harold and wished she had her phone to capture the look on his face. "There's another drawer under the family room couch, two more under the beds in the guest bedrooms, and walls of hidden food, propane canisters, candles, matches, and solar panel kits for charging our phones, in my garden shed."

"How?" Harold stammered, still in shock.

"Why don't you fire up the barbecue, and we'll cook up some hamburgers and steaks, and I'll tell you all about it over lunch?"

Dumbstruck, Harold turned to leave but then stopped. "Who are you?" he asked in awe.

Frannie reveled in the glow of his admiration for a few seconds before answering. "I'm a prepper."

Ω

OVERHEARD

Laptop open, angled away from the glare of the floor to ceiling windows, Lloyd takes a sip of his Sumatra dark roast with one packet of sugar and no cream. He inhales deeply the bold, robust aroma before setting the ceramic mug exactly six inches from the keyboard— close enough to easily retrieve, far enough away in case of an accident.

Positioned at the end of a long bench seat with an equally long table, Lloyd has the optimal view of the entire cafe, with its overstuffed chairs gathered like old friends in circles throughout the living-room style coffeehouse. The line, that extends from the cash register to just inside the door, passes in front of him like rush hour traffic—painfully slow—gives him access to snippets of conversation.

He adjusts his heavy black frames that press down on his nose before raising his hands slightly above the keyboard like a conductor pausing before the start of a symphony. Customers standing silently in line hypnotized by their phones annoy him and waste his time.

Move along.

The line inches forward without a word spoken or recorded.

A tinkle of the bell over the door alerts Lloyd to the arrival of new coffee aficionados. A gaggle of teenage girls chattering away maneuvers to the end of the line.

Finally. Something interesting.

He strains to hear their conversation delivered rapid fire and types furiously to keep up.

Girl one: "I can't believe he said that. In front of my mother!"

Girl two: "But your mom knows you're on birth control, right?"

Girl one: "Maybe? She has to know, right? I'm 17. Does she think I'm a virgin?"

The third girl who hasn't said anything up until now, pipes in. "All parents think their daughters are virgins, especially their dads."

Girl two: "True that." The other two girls laugh.

True that? What kind of slang is this?

The girls move up and are right in front of Lloyd. Their conversation has changed to what drink they are going to order.

Boring.

The sound of the bell draws Lloyd's attention to the door. A man in a charcoal gray suit enters, his phone pressed to his ear. He's speaking loud enough that the girls turn around to see who is speaking. Not finding a hot teenage boy, they turn back in unison. Lloyd doesn't need to strain to hear the conversation.

"I told them to move the meeting up a day." Pause. "It's what the client wants, so let's make it happen." Pause. "Just move the other meetings or cancel them. I don't care. Just make it happen." Heavy sigh. "I'll be in around 10." Pause. "Thanks."

The man moves up in line. He glances over at Lloyd before returning his attention back to his phone and tapping in a new number. "Tina. I'm free for the next hour. Do you want to meet?"

Maybe Tina will come here. That could be interesting. Lloyd's fingers freeze above the keys, awaiting the rest of the conversation.

"Great. The usual place? I've only got an hour." Pause. "Yes, soon. I promise. I miss you, too."

Definitely an affair. Too bad they aren't meeting here. I'd like to be privy to that *conversation.*

For the next hour, Lloyd records random snippets of conversation from the strangers who walk through the door… a frantic mom juggling her purse, phone and baby; two female joggers trying to figure out if they burned enough calories to allow for a cinnamon roll; a young guy with a skateboard flirting with the woman twice his age in line behind him. At the end of the hour, he hits save and finishes the last of his coffee before sliding his laptop into his leather bag. He leaves precisely at 9:15 and is home by 9:30 where he sets up his laptop to review the "Easter Eggs" he's collected. From 9:30 to 10:30, he weaves the bits and pieces of conversation into his story. At 10:30 his alarm reminds him it's time to go. Back out the door once more, this time to his car for the half hour drive to the office, where he works as an actuary for a private investment firm assessing and managing financial risk.

He has arranged his work schedule to start at eleven on Mondays, Wednesdays and Fridays to accommodate his "project." While numbers are his bread and butter, words are his dessert. He had the idea for the project while waiting for a plane surrounded by other passengers. The conversations humming around him were fascinating. Little slices of people's life. He found himself filling in the blanks and creating stories around what he heard. The guy in the beanie was running from the law and saying goodbye to his girlfriend. The mom with two young children and a baby in a backpack was escaping her abusive husband and fleeing for her life. The two businessmen having a heated discussion in harsh whispers were competing salesmen vying for their boss's approval.

Lloyd enjoyed making up the situations based on what he heard and decided he could write a novel, based on the conversations he recorded. Lloyd never did anything halfway. By his calculations, he'd have a finished manuscript in two months.

***

It's Wednesday... day thirteen of his twenty-four-day project. Opening the door, a brisk wind pushes fall leaves past his feet and into the café, momentarily distracting him. He steps to the right, past the line, to place his laptop on the table only to find someone else sitting in his place. Words fail him.

Sitting in his exact spot, is a woman, he guesses in her thirties, with brassy blonde hair with purple streaks. She, too, has a laptop, and is tapping away at the keys.

Lloyd clears this throat. "Excuse me."

Blue eyes lift. She looks Lloyd up and down. "Yeah."

"You're in my spot."

A wry smile spreads across her face. "Oh, really." She looks around the table. "I don't see your name anywhere." She returns to her keyboard, ignoring him.

Lloyd takes a step closer, until his thighs are pressed against the edge of the table. "I have been coming her for over a month. Every Monday, Wednesday, and Friday. Ask anyone. This is where I sit."

Without looking up. "Well, not today." Her fingers tap out a sentence.

Lloyd turns sharply and walks to the counter. "Missy. Is Greg around? I have an issue. Someone is sitting in my corner."

Missy, the twenty-something barista with a nose ring, and dyed flaming red hair, leans to the right to look around Lloyd at the woman in the corner. "Oh, her. She comes every day. She's working on a novel." Missy leans forward and whispers to Lloyd. "She collecting what people are saying while they are here. It's that interesting?"

"What?" Lloyd blasts, causing Missy to jump. "That's impossible."

With an abrupt about face, Lloyd marches over to the long table, pulls out a chair, and plants himself directly in front of the woman. "I hear you are writing a novel," he says, trying and failing to keep the venom out of his voice.

"Maybe I am, maybe I'm not. I haven't decided yet." She types.

"What's it about?" Lloyd asks, watching as her fingers move.

"Nothing in particular. Slice of life. You wouldn't be interested." More typing.

"Oh, I'm interested. I've very interested. And you know why?" Lloyd leans forward and whispers, "Because I'm writing a novel. A slice of life. Based on conversations I hear at this coffee shop, and I've been doing it for over a month. It's my idea."

It takes a moment for the woman to finish typing and look up. "Well, isn't that interesting."

"You need to move. This is where I always sit. I can hear everything from here."

A smile and a rush of fingers on the keyboard. "Yes. I know. That's why I picked it. I didn't see you here on Tuesday or on the weekend."

"Are you taking down this conversation?"

More typing. "What if I am?"

"Well, stop it. I don't want to be in your book," Lloyd says, watching as the woman types his response.

Lloyd shifts his weight from foot to foot.

What should I do? How can I demand she stop what she's doing when I've been doing the exact same thing?

The bell on the door tinkles and the businessman from the other day enters ... on the phone again. Lloyd wonders if he should continue the discussion or open his laptop. The businessman is chewing out someone and Lloyd is missing it. The woman is typing. She looks over her laptop, leans in and whispers, "I think this guy is having an affair. Juicy."

Rage flows like lava through Lloyd's veins.

He's my businessman. Mine.

Lloyd opens his laptop and a new document. The businessman moves up in line until he is standing behind Lloyd. He's talking so loudly everyone can hear him. Both Lloyd and the woman's fingers fly, struggling to keep up with the tirade. Suddenly the call is over, and The Suit, as Lloyd has named him in his novel, stuffs his phone in his back pocket and steps forward again.

Lloyd looks up. The woman takes a sip of her flavored coffee drink, pumpkin spice by the smell of it. He watches as she tucks a purple strand of hair behind her ear, revealing a large silver hoop earring. The overhead light reflects off the silver rings that adorn every finger.

Staring at his own hands, poised over the keyboard, he finds no wedding band, no rings, not even a watch. Looking up, he finds the woman is staring at him. "I'm Amber."

"Lloyd," he says begrudgingly.

He doesn't want to be friends with this woman. She burst the bright, shiny bubble of his brilliant, unique concept for a novel.

How unique can it be if this woman, this Amber person, has had the same idea?

Two teenage boys enter. Amber leans forward. "These two are very talkative. I hope you can type like the wind." She gives him a wink.

Just watch me.

The teens seem to be discussing a recent drug purchase. Who sold it to them, how much they paid, the quality, and then on and on about the great high they each had. Lloyd struggles to keep up. By the time the teens reach the register and place their order, Lloyd has written an entire page.

The duel continues between Amber and Lloyd until the phone pings, signaling that it's time for Lloyd to leave. Hitting *Save*, Lloyd closes his laptop and stands.

"Leaving so soon?" Amber quips. "You're going to miss so much."

"Some people have to work," Lloyd throws back.

"I am working. I guess what you're doing is just a hobby. See you tomorrow?"

Lloyd slips his laptop into his bag and leaves without a word.

"Bye-bye now," Amber calls out after him in a sing-song voice that makes Lloyd bristle like a dog ready to attack.

***

Friday morning, Lloyd arrives an hour earlier and finds his spot unoccupied. The satisfaction he feels of reclaiming his proper place is as rich and warm as his Sumatra blend. He sets up his laptop and places the leather satchel on the table as a buffer zone, before heading to the counter with his ceramic mug.

He enjoys a full thirty minutes of uninterrupted bliss, although it's not a productive thirty minutes. The early morning coffee drinkers are barely awake as they sleepwalk to the register for their morning addiction to kick-start their day. He had only recorded one snippet of a conversation about the change in the weather— would they get snow before Thanksgiving—the usual drivel that would never make it into his book, when Amber walks through the door. She sees him immediately and with an arched eyebrow, acknowledges that he's beaten her to the prime location.

The joy Lloyd feels is out of proportion with the small victory. *The early bird catches the worm.*

His joy is quickly vanquished when Amber places her laptop next to Lloyd's satchel, before returning to her place in line. The smile slides off Lloyd's face.

She can't be serious.

But she is and returns with her flavored drink that has more in common with a milk shake than a cup of coffee. She slides onto the bench seat and inches her way closer and closer until Lloyd catches the floral scent of her perfume.

"Really. Could you get any closer?" Lloyd asks, giving her his best scowl, which she misses as she turns on her computer.

"I think I could but then I'd be sitting in your lap. Are you sure that's what you want?" Turning, she gives him a coquettish grin, tilting her head slightly, her upper body angled just enough so that Lloyd has a full view of her ample breasts peeking over the top of a V-Neck sweater.

Smartass.

Heat simmers under Lloyd's collar. He turns away and concentrates on the blank page on the screen.

A group of high school students enter the coffee shop, excitedly chatting about the upcoming football game, including some juicy tidbits about the star quarterback and which cheerleader he was asking to the prom. Amber and Lloyd tap away, capturing the conversation.

Once the students leave, Amber takes a sip of her drink, an "ahhh" escaping her lips. "That was a good one, don't you think?"

Lloyd makes a non-committal grunt and picks up his mug to avoid saying more.

***

The following Monday, Lloyd arrives promptly at seven and beats Amber to the prime location. On Wednesday, he finds Amber has arrived before him and has won the coveted seat. She waves and yawns as he walks in. Friday morning, Lloyd waits for the door to be unlocked at six, taking great pleasure in waving to Amber when she finally arrives at seven.

A week later, Lloyd drags himself out of bed at five, in order to be at the coffee shop when it opens. Now, secure in his corner spot, holding his mug of coffee, he doesn't even open his computer. The early morning crowd, those hustling in before work, don't talk much, so there is nothing to record. With every tinkle of the bell, Lloyd's head turns in anticipation, a feeling of disappointment when Amber doesn't appear. By eight, his disappointment turns to worry.

She should be here by now.

By nine he is done. He waves a goodbye to the staff and heads out the door. He pauses to scan the cars in the parking lot. A useless endeavor, since he doesn't know what kind of car Amber drives or whether she walks or rides a bike. Once home, he doesn't bother to work on his novel. His mind is too occupied with questions.

Why didn't she show up today? Is she sick ... hurt? Maybe she's finished her book. She does visit the shop every day. What if she publishes before me? It will seem like I've copied her. I wonder what she is doing with the conversations she records. What kind of book will it be? Will it be better than mine?

It's Wednesday morning. Lloyd has been sitting in his spot for two hours when Amber walks through the door. She smiles and waves to Lloyd as she enters the line.

Coffee in hand, she slides over on the bench seat, sets down her drink and opens her laptop.

Without preamble, Lloyd blurts out, "Where were you on Monday?"

Amber turns to face Lloyd. She is wearing a soft cashmere sweater. Lloyd's eyes are drawn to evidence that she is cold and not wearing a bra. When he brings his attention to Amber's face, she wears a knowing smile.

"Hmmm. Let me see. Monday. I had an appointment. Why? Did you miss me?"

Lloyd shakes his head. "I thought you were sick or something. The staff said you hadn't been in over the weekend either."

"You were worried about me. That's sweet," she says, looking directly into his eyes, daring him to look away, which he does, mumbling something about not being worried.

After an hour of writing, Lloyd's phone pings and he closes his computer. Amber has to slide out of the way for Lloyd to leave. Before heading to the door, he says, "See you Friday?" He finds himself holding his breath waiting for her answer.

"Sure. But I won't be here until 8:00, so you can stop arriving so early. I don't care about the 'prime spot.' You can have it."

Lloyd's first thought is, *I won*, which he thought would have filled him with joy. It is a surprise to discover that the 'prime spot' doesn't matter to him after all. What matters is that Amber will be here.

Keeping his tone casual, Lloyd tosses out a, "See you on Friday, then," before walking out the door.

***

Friday finds Lloyd settled in his spot by eight, laptop open, mug filled, and a pumpkin spice latte placed to his right. Amber arrives at ten after and steps into the line.

Lloyd lifts the cup. "You don't have to wait. I bought your drink today."

Amber steps out of line and scoots along the bench seat. "Well, isn't that nice." She takes her first sip. "Perfect. How did you know what I like?"

Lloyd shrugs. "I asked Missy to make me your usual, soy milk and all."

Amber gives him an appreciative nod. She leans toward him. "Is that aftershave I smell?"

Lloyd is both pleased and embarrassed that she noticed. "Just a little something I splashed on."

"I like it."

Before they could say more, a group of talkative women enter. Lloyd and Amber look at each other, a knowing smile passing between them, before they begin typing. It turns out to be an exceptional morning. Everyone seems to be in good spirits, chatting about everything from the price of gas to the new movie premiering at the local theater.

By the time Lloyd's phone pings, he has filled seven pages with conversations. Instead of standing to leave, he shuts off his computer and turns to Amber. "I was wondering... what is your novel about?"

Amber turns completely to face Lloyd. "Do you really want to know? I mean, the last time I talked about it, you seemed very upset."

"I was upset. Now I'm more curious than upset," Lloyd admits.

"First off, I'm not writing a novel. It's a compilation of short stories called *Conversations at a Coffeehouse*. How about you? What is your book about?"

Knowing she isn't writing a novel, lifts a weight off of Lloyd's shoulders. "I'm writing a novel called, *The Community*. I follow the lives of several characters and how they all interact in the coffee shop… The Suit, the Teens, the Moms, the Girls.

"We're taking the same conversations but using them differently. Interesting."

Interesting, but not as interesting as you.

"Can I take you out to dinner?" Lloyd blurts out.

"It's a bit early for dinner," Amber teases.

"I mean, later. Can I take you out to dinner tonight?" Lloyd asks more slowly.

"Finally. I thought you'd never ask," she says, a mischievous twinkle in her eyes.

Lloyd is confused. "Wait. What? You've been waiting for me to ask you out?"

"Come on. You don't think I really cared about sitting in your spot, do you? And I certainly didn't enjoy waking up before seven just to beat you here. I'm not really a morning person and that was killing me."

"Me, too. By two o'clock I needed another two cups of coffee to make it to quitting time. So why did you do it?" Lloyd asks.

"I enjoyed seeing your frustration when you arrived and found me in your place. I enjoyed watching you squirm as I moved into your personal space. And I really got a kick out of watching you fall for me."

Lloyd leans in, her perfume intoxicating, her smile unravels him. "So, you were just messing with me."

Amber nods.

"I'm not sure what I'm getting myself into."

Amber laughs and it sounds the same as the tinkle of the bell on the door. "Oh, I think you do."

Ω

**Thank you for reading.
I hope you enjoyed these
slice of life stories.**